CHOOSING EDEN

WHEN CHOOSING IS NOT A CHOICE

A SEAHORSE ISLAND NOVEL
BOOK TWO

LISA LEE

Choosing Eden

A SEAHORSE ISLAND NOVEL

BOOK TWO: **WHEN CHOOSING IS NOT A CHOICE**

LISA LEE

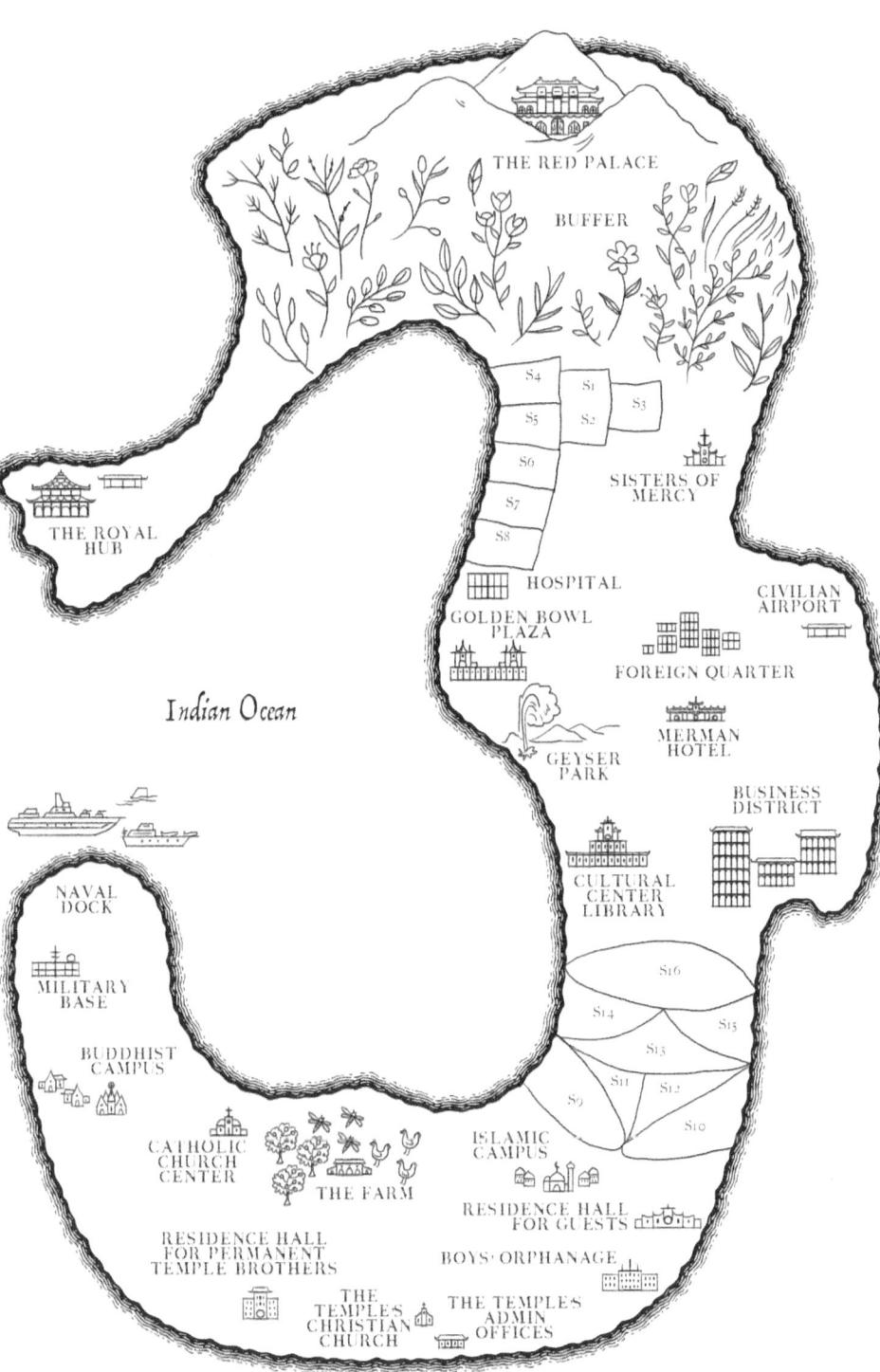

CONTENTS

ISBN 978-1-7326290-2-8 (EBOOK)

ISBN 978-1-7326290-3-5 (PAPERBACK)

This is a work of fiction. Names, characters, businesses, places, events, locales, and incidents are either the products of the author's imagination or used in a fictitious manner. Any resemblance to actual persons, living or dead, or actual events is purely coincidental.

Cover Design and Illustration by Patricia Moffett

Formatting by Patricia Moffett

Printed in the United States of America

First Printing February 2024

Published by Lisa Lee

Chicago, IL

Lisaleewrites18@gmail.com

www.LisaLeeWrites.com

"Love is not love
Which alters when it alteration finds,
Or bends with the remover to remove.
O no! it is an ever-fixed mark
That looks on tempests and is never shaken;
It is the star to every wand'ring bark,
Whose worth's unknown, although his height be taken."
Excerpted from Sonnet 116 by William Shakespeare

"It was but a little that I passed from them, but I found him whom my soul loveth: I held him, and would not let him go, until I had brought him into my mother's house, and into the chamber of her that conceived me."
Bible, Song of Solomon 3:4 (KJV)

EDEN, A RAY OF HOPE

When I imagined meeting the man who purchased me as his bride, I never thought about what I would wear or how I would look. After two-plus years of attending the Joseph Hyde School for Exceptional Girls, I knew all I cared to know about hairstyles, makeup, and clothes. Not to say I was an expert by any means, but I just kind of assumed I would be dressed appropriately for such an auspicious occasion.

My concern was more about the man I would be marrying. Until I was nearly fourteen, I had blissfully assumed I would one day meet the boy of my dreams and we would fall in love, get married, and live happily ever after in Sunny City, New Jersey. Spoiler alert, that's not what happened. Instead, for reasons I won't reminisce about, I was kidnapped—a quite awful experience—and taken to a secretive boarding school where I learned that my graduation gift was to be married to the man who purchased me. Oh, and to make matters even better, I would have no contact with this man or any member of my family for the entire four years of schooling. That lovely plan didn't pan out either. It was not even halfway through my junior year, and my intended groom stood towering over me.

"My bride, I presume," he said as he reached out his right hand to help me up from where I lay face down on the ground. His left hand held a long rifle.

I half-turned, intending to raise myself to at least a sitting position, but had to pause after the movement. My body was coming out of shock mode, reminding me of all the bruises and aches. So instead of taking his hand, I stared up at him silently.

His tall muscular form, clothed in blood-spattered fatigues and black combat boots, appeared to have risen out of the ground like some sort of night golem. The metallic smell of blood reached my flared nostrils, the scent so strong I could almost taste the iron in my mouth.

I swallowed dryness. The only thing tethering me to reality was the kindness, or what I took for kindness, in his eyes and face. But then the soldiers nearest him moved away, shining their flashlights on other prey, and night reasserted its darkness.

The friendly gaze disappeared into a menacing shadow. Are shadows ever not menacing? Even the moon shied away from him, instead illuminating me in all my ignominy. From where I lay on the chilled dirt, I used my hands to push the upper part of my body off the ground. As I tried to move upward, my brain felt as if it were two seconds behind the rest of me. A minor delay except for the headache that mushroomed, bringing along nausea and pain. I wondered fleetingly if I had a concussion.

Turning away from the hand offered by my presumed groom, I propped my arms to keep my torso raised. Before I could look back up, my eyes involuntarily widened at the soiled state of my dress. When the flight attendant presented me with the dress and suggested I freshen up before I deplaned, I had been sinfully awed by its beauty. The sleeveless dress was made of creamy blue silk and ruffled around the edges. But now the beautiful dress was torn and covered with dirt, my hair was falling out of its proper bun, and my ankle lay twisted in my new medium-height heels. In fact, everything on my left side hurt—my jaw, side, and leg. My hands clenched the dirt to hold back the pain. I was completely unpresentable but determined not to further humiliate myself by sobbing.

My groom barked an order to another soldier, handed over his gun, and squatted in front of me. "Eden," he said, "I'm so very sorry."

Now that I could see his face more clearly again, I hoped the concern and kindness I saw on it were genuine. While clearly older than me, he was still young, which surprised me.

"What . . . what happened?" I stammered out the question. I had thought I was arriving someplace safer than the one I left. Instead, before I could even take two steps out of the car, I'd been thrown and tackled. I had struggled against whoever it was that had pinned me to the ground, unwilling to let myself be taken as easily as I had the first time. But the man in front of me had come to my aid, removing my attacker.

"The family was betrayed," my groom replied grimly. "Trust me; they will pay for what happened here today. But right now, you look like you will faint on the ground. Let's get medical over here." He stood again.

Pathetically, I panicked at the thought of being left on the ground by myself, but then he signaled someone to come over. I braced my wobbly arms, silently telling my disbelieving body to rise.

"I thought," I began before pausing as pain sliced through me. "I thought you would be older." I cringed inwardly, wishing my first words to him were more sophisticated.

"You did?" he asked, surprised.

I nodded in reply but didn't speak. I had imagined my husband-to-be was someone old and unpleasant. Why else would he need to pay for a bride? It made no sense that the man still looming over me was my groom.

"Did you think you were marrying my brother?" he asked, looking down at me with a raised eyebrow. "He's already married. Besides, I'm only younger by fifteen minutes." To my relief, he grinned, his white teeth cutting through the darkness of night.

I smiled back before I realized what I was doing. Unsure of what to say, I turned my head toward nearby voices. A group of four soldiers was carrying a stretcher.

"Don't look," said my groom, his voice harsh, his playful smile gone. He had crouched in front of me again.

3

Of course, I looked. At first, I didn't comprehend what I was seeing. The soldiers seemed to be carrying something covered by a white sheet.

My groom reached out toward me, and I flinched away, residual shock giving way to the ever-present fear of what steps were next on this unplanned journey. I could hear my mother say, "Eden, don't run from the frying pan to the fire." Thinking of my mom and her recent death ripped the minuscule amount of remaining bravado right out of me. I stared at the ground as my whole body began to shake, including my fingers anchored determinedly in the ground.

"I didn't mean to scare you," my groom said gently. "I just wanted to cover your eyes, so you didn't have to see the body."

What body? I wondered, my head spinning as I remembered the blood on his boots and the loud booms when I was tackled to the ground. Were those gunshots?

All my wondering stopped when I saw an arm fall from the side of the stretcher as it went past me. I recognized the silver bracelet around the wrist. The bracelet belonged to Mr. Holmes, the man who had driven me to this eerie estate hidden away in the woods of the UK. I gasped as I realized he was now dead. Had he been a friend or foe? What about the other men traveling with us? It was then that I noticed how cold I was. Sleeveless silk was not the best choice for a fall evening in the UK.

"Wh-what happened to the other men with him?" I asked, my teeth chattering as I rubbed my arms for warmth.

His averted gaze told me what I had not truly wanted to know. I shivered as knowledge made the autumn chill a sharpened blade of unbreakable ice.

"Get me a goddamn blanket right now!" my groom yelled as I fell back fully to the ground. It seemed as if only moments ago, I had luxuriated in the night sky, the full heavy moon and stars that blinked as if harbingers of good fortune. But now, my tender psyche was overrun by the night's events and everything that had led up to them. Above me, everything blurred—the moon, stars, clouds, and his face. I closed my eyes against such disorder.

"Get medical," he ordered.

"On their way, but I have a heated blanket," said another voice, softer, feminine.

A warm blanket covered me, the heat warming up all the cold spots within me. Despite the pain from my injuries, the heat made me drowsy, and I gave in to the oblivion of sleep.

WHEN CONSCIOUSNESS RETURNED, I lay still. As the seconds ticked by, I heard nothing except the sound of my own breathing. The silence coiled around me, languidly at first but then suddenly becoming tighter and tighter until the state of unknowing became untenable.

Taking a deep breath, I gingerly opened my eyes, wincing as bright, piercing sunlight streamed directly on my face. I held up a hand to shield my eyes, but something felt off. My left hand was wrapped in some sort of soft gauze, and little wires were connected to various parts of my chest, wrists, and arms.

Startled, I sat up and started patting myself as I realized my clothes had been replaced with a white gown, the word "hospital" written all over it in pink lettering. Exploring the left side of my body, I could feel bandages through the gown. My left ankle was wrapped in some sort of brace. I was quite disconcerted to realize that without my consent or knowledge, someone had undressed me, treated my scrapes and wounds, and dressed me again.

There was no sense of time passing. It seemed but a moment ago I was lying on the ground in pain, cold and afraid. Now, I lay in a bed with handrails in a huge room. I would have assumed I was in an infirmary or hospital, but my bed was the only one. The rest of the space was ostentatiously cavernous.

My attention was caught by the overlarge chandelier as it strained against the metal rope anchoring it. The fixture was comprised of long, thin sheets of metal placed at odd angles, barely allowing any light to get through from the light source at its center. So ugly was the fixture that I blinked several times to make sure I wasn't dreaming or, rather, having a nightmare.

Once I realized the curtain had closed on dreamland, I looked with more interest at my surroundings. To my left, bright sunlight streamed through the glass at the top of the wall, but a heavy curtain shrouded the rest of the glass down to the floor. Based on the metal that divided the glass, or at least the part I could see of it, I figured the glass was actually two halves of a sliding door. My injured ankle twitched, and I was surprised by my hunger to see what was on the other side of the curtain. Perhaps a balcony or a garden?

A door opening turned my attention back to the inside of the room, and two women in police gear entered and stood on either side of the door on the wall adjacent to the wall with the curtained windows. They gave me a quick nod and stared impassively ahead, ignoring my gaping mouth, and I belatedly remembered to close it. Why would women be dressed as police officers?

Then I remembered the female doctor I had in Untouchable City, where the normal rules didn't apply. This place must be like Untouchable City, where women had more options, meaning I was in a hospital room with real police officers guarding the door.

I stiffened as I wondered why they were present. Fear, always lurking within me, awoke from its slumber, a slithering snake poised to strike. But then the door opened again, and a woman who appeared only a few years older than me burst into the room. She stopped right inside the door as she noticed me.

"You're awake!" she practically shouted and hurried over to me. "I'm Nurse Summers. The doctor will be in soon. Sorry for the delay. It's been crazy busy."

Here she paused to take my wrist, presumably to take my pulse. She wore a crisp and blindingly white uniform, completely at odds with her choppy-cut purple hair. After she keyed in something on her electronic notepad, she continued chatting, smoothing the sheets and blanket on the bed.

"You know, Princess Charlotte had her baby this morning, so the media is swarming all over. Plus, there was a pileup on London Road, and the public hospital overflowed, so we were ordered to take in the extra. If you ask me, they should build another public hospital. No sense—"

A cough from one of the officers made the nurse pause. She then unrepentantly winked at me and said, "Sorry, luv. Can't talk politics with our diplomatic guests. Not that I was talking politics, just common sense—"

Another discreet cough from the officer brought an eye roll and a sigh from her. "Any who, those are your guards over there, Sergeant Thomas and Sergeant Evans. I heard the Sorean prince insisted on security, and our queen agreed. I guess trying to keep the peace between countries and whatnot."

Not a cough this time, but a suggestion came from the other sergeant. "I don't believe Ms. Edwards has eaten yet."

Okay, I thought to myself. *I must still be in England. The sergeants and the purple-haired nurse sound just like the folks at the airport yesterday. And Princess Charlotte is definitely British, right?*

"Push the menu button on your remote," Nurse Summers said, interrupting my internal dialogue as she reached over to readjust the wires sticking to my upper chest. "You hungry?"

I nodded as I fumbled with the remote. I couldn't help a tiny gasp of surprise when I realized the still-life poster on the wall opposite me was a screen.

"How's your pain level?"

"I'm fine," I said, surprising myself with the truth of my reply. Except for a mild twinge here and there, my pain was a lot less than the night before. My throat, however, was parched. I pushed the button for orange juice as I swallowed to soothe my throat.

"Your doctor should be in shortly. She got held up with another patient. There's a male doctor, but I heard you're from Saved America, so you can only have female doctors?" Here, Nurse Summers looked at me with a question in her eyes. I looked at the sergeants, but they just looked at each other, apparently trying to decide if this question was appropriate or not.

I tried to think of how to answer, but Nurse Summers didn't wait for a response. "Don't worry about it. I suppose I can't ask if you and the prince are an item, but that is one fine—"

"I think that's enough, nurse." A tall man stood at the door, his white doctor's coat swamping his thin frame. His furrowed brow and pinched expression revealed his displeasure. I felt guilty even though I knew he meant the admonishment for Nurse Summers.

"That man is not a doctor in the hospital!" Nurse Summers shouted, pressing a bright red button on the wall near my bed.

Strobe lights started flashing in the ceiling and the floor, while an alarm blared loud enough to hurt my eardrums. The intruder's face turned ugly, his lip curling in disgust as he lunged at me.

Without thinking, I slid off the bed on the other side. My legs immediately buckled, and I fell onto my hands and knees. I half-crawled, half-dragged myself toward the curtained glass doors in front of me, ignoring the brace on my left ankle. I might have a chance of survival outside, if the glass wasn't a window from which I would fall to my death. I consciously let go of the frightening thought and tried to hurry, but I was uncoordinated and slow.

Halfway between the bed and the glass doors, I heard a loud crash and then something pushed into me from behind. I slid into the glass doors, nearly bumping my head until I put my hand out to catch myself. When I turned, the police sergeants had the intruder on the floor, one of them straddling his back as she put handcuffs on him. He tried to buck her off, but she took his head and slammed it into the floor.

"Stay down," she yelled.

As though conjured with her shout, a bunch of guards entered the room, their heavy black boots stomping the floor. They wore all-black bulky gear making their bodies seem larger, more threatening. The officers took the man away, his bloodied face glaring back at me with such malevolence that I shivered.

After the door closed on his visage, the room promptly emptied with just a few officers remaining. Almost immediately, though, the room filled with medical staff trying to set the room to rights.

I had the hysterical thought, *First black coats, then white coats.* I wanted to laugh, but I knew I couldn't. I clenched my hands together to stifle the inappropriate laughter bubbling within me. As I sat on the floor with my back against the glass windows, I took some comfort in the warmth seeping in from the sun-warmed glass.

"Miss, we'll need a statement," a hard, implacable voice said. An officer squatted in front of me, much like my groom had the night before, but instead of kind eyes and friendly words, the man in front of me had dead eyes and a tone that told me he wouldn't really understand anything I said. His whole demeanor made me recoil, and I turned my head away.

An arm came around me. Startled, I whipped my head around, expecting to see the officer, but instead, it was Nurse Summers, sitting on the ground with me. But she wasn't looking at me. "Officer," she began.

"It's captain," he stated in a clipped tone.

"Oh, sorry, captain," she said, her derisive tone negating her apology. "You know as well as I do that you have to wait for the diplomatic liaison to arrive before you question her. A hospital VP is on the way and will wait with her until the liaison arrives." The two looked at each other before he sighed and stood.

He couldn't avoid one last parting shot. "If the hospital security was doing its job, this wouldn't have happened. Now, even though we're stretched, I have to assign officers to figure out what happened here."

"Yes, you do," another hard voice said, but this time it came from my groom, apparently a prince if I understood Nurse Summers's comment correctly.

If my life were a fairytale, the prince and I would have fallen in love —or at least like—at first sight and all my problems would have been solved by coy eyes and fluttering hearts. But what princess-to-be had problems like mine?

No amount of love could fill the vast void within me, the warmth that once existed viciously clawed out by loss upon loss. I had lost my family and friends. I knew for sure my mother was dead. The others, I could only guess whether they were alive or dead, but I doubted I would ever see them again. I had tried to hold on to hope and faith, but it was like holding on to air. Having someone try to kill me twice in less than twenty-four hours took whatever core of me was left. I was shattering into a million pieces and no longer cared about the whys of my life.

As further evidence that my life was not a warm, fuzzy story, the prince completely ignored me as he spoke with security personnel. His presence made things even more frenetic than before. The room filled with more police and medical staff moving around so quickly it made me dizzy.

"Let's get you into bed," Nurse Summers murmured as she got me up with the help of another nurse. We maneuvered around the crush. My legs still felt wobbly, and the brace didn't help matters. It was a relief when we finally reached the bed.

I let go of the nurses and reached for the bed, only to be told it wasn't quite ready. The prior bed had tilted over in the scuffle and been removed. A new one had been brought in, and I watched as no fewer than five hospital staff members put on sheets and confirmed that different buttons were working. Finally, the bed was deemed ready for my presence.

"Do you want to sit up or lie down?" Nurse Summers asked as she assisted me onto the bed.

"Sit up," I replied.

"Oh look, she talks," she teased as she pressed something that made the back of the bed rise.

I looked at her blankly, not seeing the humor.

"Sorry," she said, red flushing her cheeks. "Let me reattach the wires and go check your chart."

With her gone, it felt as if my last war ally had deserted me. The room was filled with people with whom I had no connection. What about the man in the doctor's coat who had tried to kill me? Did he have friends who remained in the hospital, waiting for another chance to strike?

As I looked around the room, all I saw were the cold smiles of the medical staff or the expressionless faces of security and police. I wanted to run out of the room to escape their collective gaze. But where would I go? Who could I trust?

Tears of frustration pricked at my eyelids, and my body flushed hot with embarrassment as I looked down at the sheets. I simultaneously hoped that my unbound hair shielded most of my face and that it wasn't completely wild. My curls had a life of their own and were hard to tame on the best of days. This day wasn't even a semi-good one, not unless you counted my being alive as good. Wait, being alive was good. Never mind.

A movement to my left interrupted the philosophical debate with myself. I pushed a mass of kinky-curly hair behind my left ear and glanced sideways, to see the prince's sympathetic gaze looking back at me.

"Excuse me, everyone," the prince said. "I would like a moment alone with Ms. Edwards."

Just like that, the room cleared, only the prince and me remaining. Well, the two female police sergeants took up their spots by the door again, but otherwise, the room was clear.

The prince turned to look at the sergeants, who both nodded once before stepping outside. The one on the left, Sergeant Evans I think, mentioned that they would be stationed just outside the door. I got the impression that she would not hesitate to run back in if there were any problems.

I turned my gaze from the door to find the prince looking at me. "I thought you needed a moment alone," he said with a droll smile.

I nodded as I let out a breath I didn't know I was holding.

"Thank you," I said in Sorean, my voice a little hoarse. I had never received the orange juice I ordered.

The prince's face lit up when he heard me speaking Sorean. He spoke it back to me but not in the hesitant way I had. Instead, I got a torrent of Sorean coming so fast that I completely lost what he was saying after the first sentence or two. My expression must have shown my confusion because he broke off mid-sentence.

"I lost you," he said in English with a wry grin. "I'll switch back to English."

I nodded to show that I understood him.

"I was saying that the island has had a problem with the terrorist group Seven," he continued. "We got most of them a couple of years ago but not all. I'm afraid they may have rebuilt their numbers, but today's attack on you may lead us to them."

He began pacing back and forth by the side of my bed, his black dress shoes clipping rhythmically against the tile floor. "I can't believe they attacked here!" He stopped and pulled out his phone and again spoke in rapid Sorean. He didn't wait for a response but instead hung up before the other person responded.

"That's taken care of," he said as he turned back to me. "I promise you we will get to the bottom of this situation, but we may have to leave for the island earlier than I planned."

"Seahorse Island?" I asked.

He stared at me for a moment before smiling and shaking his head.

"We'll start over," he said. "I am Prince Gideon Li from Seahorse Island, son of King Edward Li and Queen Jasmine Li, and younger brother, by mere minutes, to Prince Gabriel Li."

A prince? Nurse Summers was right. He really was a prince. But why was I marrying a prince? I puzzled over this question before realizing that the prince in question was looking at me expectantly but somewhat resigned.

"Oh! I'm sorry," I said as I remembered my manners. "My name is Eden Edwina Edwards from Sunny City, New Jersey, in Saved America, daughter of . . . daughter of . . ." Feeling my hoarse voice start to tremble, I ended without finishing the introduction.

Before I could get inside my head and agonize over the introduction, his hand covered mine. "You lost your parents?" he said, his voice a soft bass.

"My mom," I said unsteadily. *One lost, one dead,* I thought but didn't trust my voice to explain.

"I'm sorry," he said as his hand tightened on mine. "Your father?"

I shook my head and lowered my gaze.

"I guess that explains things," he mused.

"Huh?" I queried, not sure if he was talking to me or not. Yes, I did take the Art of Conversation classes, but apparently, my learning deserted me during times of stress.

"My parents are set on you being my bride," he said with a sigh, still holding my hand.

"Why?" I asked, hoping to understand why I was chosen for someone who so obviously didn't need help finding a wife. Now, in the light of day, I could clearly see his features: black almond-shaped eyes, long nose, medium lips, chiseled cheekbones, and closely cropped black hair. His bronzed skin practically glowed in the few rays of sunlight filtering into the room. He looked like the men they had on romance novel covers at the library back in Sunny City.

I had once overheard two elderly ladies at the library complaining that romance novels no longer had any sizzle, that the inspectors had ruined them. But one of them said she still checked them out if for nothing else than just to look at the hotties on the cover. My mother had hurried me away before I could hear more.

My cheeks flushed as I thought about the man holding my hand being on the cover of one of those books. I wondered if I should swoon or something but then sobered up as I realized there was probably something majorly wrong with him if his parents felt the need to find him a bride. As he looked at me with a puzzled expression, I realized I had missed his reply.

"I'm sorry; what did you say?" I asked. I really would have to do a better job of listening.

"They have their reasons," he repeated, but his gaze, so direct up to that point, avoided mine.

"You don't want me to be your bride?" I asked, not sure how to take his evasiveness. I longed to know what it was about me that had caused the loss of everything dear in my life for the sake of marriage to the man in front of me. It couldn't be just because he was a prince.

"I just found out about you," he said with a sigh.

"What?" I asked, shocked. "I've been preparing to be married to you for over two years!"

An expression crossed his face that I couldn't read. Just short of revulsion, the cringy expression on his face looked more like distaste.

"How old are you?" he asked.

"Sixteen," I replied, trying to keep up with the flow of the conversation.

Abruptly, he dropped my hand. "I'm twenty-five."

I nodded, sensing he was finally going somewhere with this thread of the conversation.

Before he could respond, there was a knock on the door. He went over and sent whoever it was away before speaking briefly to the sergeants, who remained just outside the room.

As he walked back to the bed, I noticed how different he looked in the black suit compared to the fatigues he had been wearing before. Yesterday, he had seemed muscled and massive to me. Today, the black suit with the black silk shirt left unbuttoned at the collar gave him a much sleeker look. I momentarily wondered if the silk was real or just a good imitation.

"Look, we don't have much time before the doctor comes in," he began. "Once we get to the island—yes, we are going to Seahorse Island —you will become a ward of my family. This means you will be under the protection of the Royal Family Li. After seven years, if we suit, we'll get married. If not, we find other partners to marry. Does that sound like a deal?"

As I stared up at Prince Gideon, a missing key slipped into place. In my junior year at the Joseph Hyde School for Exceptional Girls, I had been assigned a new teacher to teach me the Sorean culture and language. The only issue was that the classes had to be somewhat secretive considering that the teacher, Mr. Holt, was a man and the school only allowed female teachers. I wondered if he had been sent by the royal family to prepare me for my new role.

"Do you know Jack Holt?" I asked.

"No," Prince Gideon responded with a glance at the door and a frown. "Should I?"

I shook my head. "Never mind. If I accept this deal, what do I have to do?"

"Put up with my mother," he replied with a rueful grin. "Pretend like you agree with everything she's saying on marriage."

"That's it?" I asked.

As he nodded, I bit the inside of my lip. While one key had fallen into place, I still had a lot of locks without keys. The prince's plan didn't make things any clearer for me. But it would buy me time.

His expression hardened. "Look, I have some screwed-up stuff in my past, but I will pick my own wife." He frowned. "It's surreal for me to be having this conversation with a kid."

"I'm old enough to be married," I explained. "Nine- and ten-year age gaps are not uncommon."

"In *your* country, you are old enough," he countered, not quite able to hide the judgment in his words. Was it possible to feel ashamed and relieved at the same time?

"Don't take offense," he said, reaching for me and then dropping his hand. "I don't hold your country against you," he said with a half-smile. "It's just that for a moment, I thought you were someone else, but I was mistaken."

"I see," I said, even though I really did not. "What will I do for seven years?"

"School," he replied a bit impatiently.

I kept forgetting I wasn't in Saved America anymore. I could go on to university without needing a morality inspector to recommend me. The thought released a huge weight I didn't even know I was carrying.

I had been so consumed with finding out more information about my dad and my friends and finding a new normal in which I could find a more certain rhythm to my days. But this dream I thought I had fully released was returned to me by the impatient man in front of me.

Quickly wiping away the embarrassing grateful tear that spilled down one cheek, I started to ask about my dad and my friends, but the prince's fingers had started to tap against the bed rail, and I knew I was out of time. It didn't matter. I would find a way to get the information I so desperately wanted.

"You have a deal," I said, holding out my hand to his.

He grinned that sure grin of his that almost made me smile in return. We shook hands just as the door opened. The sergeants and two new women entered. One looked to be around the prince's age, but the other was older. Neither wore a white coat.

"The nurse and doctor are conferring outside," the younger woman said as she smiled at the prince with a slight head bow. "I'm the diplomatic liaison, and this is Esther Simmons, a vice president for the hospital." The older woman's terse head nod reminded me of Mrs. Flint, the head of my old house at school.

"What?" Gideon said, frowning. "The hospital staff let you in?"

"I work for the Sorean embassy here, and the hospital staff vetted my credentials," the younger woman replied with a toss of her long straight black hair and a slightly less easy smile than before.

"Emma, cut to the chase," Gideon demanded as he pulled out his phone. "Why are you here?"

Instead of answering him, the woman named Emma turned to me with a sigh, crossed her arms across her chest, and started tapping her foot. "Ms. Edwards, I'm supposed to ask you a whole bunch of questions about how you were injured and whether you feel safe with the current adults in your life. But instead of wasting both of our time, I'm just going to ask: do you have any concerns about going with Prince Gideon to Seahorse Island?"

I opened my mouth to speak but then decided to just shake my head to indicate no. Before I finished one head shake, she had already turned her attention back to the prince. The hospital vice president's lips tightened as she made notes on her electronic notepad.

"Now, I can discuss the real issue." Wrinkling her delicate nose, Emma said, "Our media friends are speculating that she's an unsuitable lover you met on one of your secret military excursions."

Gideon and I both burst out laughing. Shocked that I could still laugh, I slapped my hand over my mouth.

"Don't worry," Gideon said with a smile. "It's quite humorous."

"Yes," Emma said. "Quite humorous." Was it only me or was there a note of disdain in her voice?

Gideon looked at her with narrowed eyes before asking, "How did the news about Eden get out?"

Emma's hand fluttered to just below her neck as she shook her head. "You let it out, sir, when you rushed into the emergency room with a bunch of soldiers crowding behind you. You couldn't have scripted a better story for the tabloids."

"You were Angel's friend," he said to her and moved closer to me, his hand resting protectively on my shoulder.

Emma jerked back as if he had slapped her. Her golden face went pale, as if the blood had been drained from it.

Confused, I turned to look at the prince, but his face was hard. The sergeants at the door seemed to tense also, their hands resting closer to their weapons. The metaphysical snake within me opened her mouth wide to feed on the fear coursing through me, only to have my actual stomach growl in hunger.

With uncanny timing, the door opened again to reveal Nurse Summers. She was holding a tray with orange juice, a small tea container, and a covered plate. The delicious aroma of the unseen food made me almost faint. I had to clench my hands together to avoid reaching for the tray.

A middle-aged, brown-skinned woman in a white doctor's coat entered right behind Nurse Summers. My eyes widened as I recognized Dr. Brown, the doctor from Untouchable City. She gave a subtle shake of her head. Following her lead, I gave no hint that I had already met her as we shook hands. After the introductions were made, the hospital vice president excused herself and left.

Dr. Brown, Nurse Summers, Prince Gideon, and Emma stood around my bed. I wanted to inhale the delicious food on the tray in front of me, but I felt awkward being watched. I also couldn't ask the questions I wanted to ask the doctor with the other folks in the room.

"I understand that you want to assure yourselves that Eden is okay, but she needs to eat and rest," Dr. Brown told the prince and Emma in a carefully polite and neutral tone. "Do you mind coming back tomorrow?"

Relieved, I finally took a sip of the orange juice. The combination of tart sweetness and cold was soothing to my parched throat.

"With everything that's happened yesterday and today," the prince said, "I would feel more comfortable if I slept on the sofa over there." He pointed in the direction of the sitting area. "Security will be here as well."

The doctor and the prince stared at each other as I held the cold glass of orange juice in my hand. The doctor's mouth thinned before she nodded her head to indicate agreement.

"Sir," Emma began.

"We'll let Eden eat," the prince said to her. "Let's go outside and discuss the statement for the media."

After they left, Dr. Brown gave me a quick examination using her stethoscope on my back and chest.

"Did the medication I gave you help?" she asked.

"You ordered medication?" Nurse Summers asked with a frown as she looked down at the electronic notepad in her hand. "I don't see it listed."

"You're right," Dr. Brown said, her hands tightening briefly on the handrails. "It's been a long day." I knew she was referring to the medications she gave me after I was rescued from the fire at my old school. Just thinking about the heat and smoke of the fire made my throat tighten.

"Everything's good," I said to Dr. Brown.

"Really?" she asked.

I nodded.

Dr. Brown sighed and shook her head. "Eat your meal and get some rest. I will be back to check in on you later tonight." She gave a quick glance at the nurse who was looking at her notepad. "We can talk more then."

I slept, but I didn't rest. My dream started as disjointed and distorted images of the past week. In the first scene, I was making barrettes in my Domestic Arts class, but instead of the cool serenity of blues and greens, my barrettes were a vivacious red, the color of happiness. Instead of my classmate Jaelle pointing out the fire, the door to the classroom opened to reveal Mrs. Flint, the head of the Jade Vine House, my house. Not unusual for her to check in on Mrs. Askew's Domestic Arts classes. Mrs. Askew was known as the laziest teacher in the entire school. What was unusual was that Prince Gideon accompanied her. He was dressed in the same black suit and shirt I had seen him in earlier that day. No one gasped in shock at a man being in the school. In fact, everyone was smiling, including my best friends, Kaitlyn and Bethany.

In my dream, I was so happy to see him that I sort of floated to him —who walks in dreams? As he enveloped me in a hug, I caught scents of bergamot and lavender. Leaning into the scent and warmth of him, I closed my eyes as the prince pulled me closer.

After a moment, I opened my eyes, only to gaze directly into the glare of Mr. Holt standing right outside the classroom door, behind the prince. His mouth was a thin slash, and his eyes flashed angrily. Oh no, I forgot about the fire. I turned to warn the others, but I was too late. Instead of my friends, all I saw was a raging inferno.

"Nooooo!" I screamed, waking myself up and startling a new pair of sergeants who looked around trying to identify the threat.

"Just a dream," I croaked.

The door opened, and Dr. Brown rushed in. As she reassured herself that I wasn't having a medical emergency, I focused on the sliver of glass shown above the curtains. It was completely dark outside. I had slept almost the entire day. I looked at the sofa, but the prince wasn't there. I wasn't sure if I was relieved or disappointed.

2

GIDEON, SOMEONE TO WATCH OVER

The plane twisted and flexed as it propelled forward furiously against a strong headwind, outrunning sound itself at sixty thousand feet above the earth. Ignoring the engineering marvel, Gideon stood to stretch his legs. They had taken off an hour before from Manchester. It was now ten at night London time, but no one was sleeping.

Luke and James were playing spades. On the other side of the aisle, the remaining three guards were playing poker using mini chocolate candies instead of money. Gideon pretended not to notice the substitution from mini whiskey bottles to chocolate after furtive whispers and glances his way.

The men were situated toward the front of the plane, but Eden sat all the way back in the second-to-last row. Her dull gaze remained locked on the darkness outside her window seat, her arms crossed in front. Sitting next to her was his surprise guest Nurse Summers. When she saw him looking back, she gave him a cheeky grin and a thumbs-up. Gideon gave her a tight head nod before sitting again with an elongated sigh.

"She checked out," James said quietly.

"I know," Gideon said. "But it will be difficult to explain her."

James shrugged. "It would have been more difficult to explain an underage female on a plane with all adult males." Turning to Luke, he said, "Are you marking the cards?"

"No," Luke retorted. "And you're wrong. The co-pilot and one of the flight attendants are 'females,' so Eden wouldn't have been the only 'female' on the plane." Luke made air quotes with his fingers.

"You are as annoying as ever!" Gideon said, irritated at how quickly Luke could get under his skin.

The conversation between the three other guards paused.

Thinking of a swear word but holding it back, Gideon turned toward the other men. "Is there a problem?"

"No, sir," the most senior one replied, and they went back to playing their game.

Gideon turned to glare at Luke, who just rolled his eyes. "News flash, you haven't changed either," Luke said.

Luke and James had been handpicked as personal guards for Gideon and his brother, Gabriel, back when they were in their teens. The twins had nicknamed the guards the Royal Snitches since it seemed their primary function was to report the brothers' misdeeds to the king. Gideon had been able to forgo the pleasure of their company for the two years he was in the military, but now he was back and stuck with them again.

"Luke, watch it," James said as he looked directly at the other guard. "We're not alone."

Luke grimaced. "Sorry, sir."

"Don't worry," Gideon said. "I'll just recommend protocol retraining class . . . again."

"Yes, sir." Luke managed to get the words out between clenched teeth.

Startled by Luke's response, Gideon laughed a humorless bark. "I can't believe you just took that statement seriously."

"Sir, you are Prince Gideon," James replied instead of Luke. "You aren't in the military anymore."

Trust James to remind him of his place. "Duly noted," Gideon said as he leaned over. "But in truth, after everything, the fact that you're still here means a lot."

Luke paused from dealing the cards to stare wide-eyed at Gideon before turning to James. In a hushed whisper, he said, "Sir, I think an imposter has replaced the prince."

Gideon gave Luke a very unroyal finger before he fully stood back up.

"Princely behavior indeed!" Luke retorted. "Why aren't you playing?" he continued as he finished dealing the cards.

Gideon shrugged before moving his upper body from side to side to loosen his back muscles. "I just want to stand for a while." Pausing in his stretching to look apologetically at Luke and James, he said, "Besides it would be like taking candy from a baby. For the last year, I was known as the King of Spades."

"King of Spades? More like the Prince of Clubs!" Luke said, almost choking on his laughter.

James tried to hold it in, but Gideon saw him turn his head, shoulders shaking.

Gideon sat down next to James and looked across the small table at Luke. "Deal again."

"Yes, sir," Luke said with a smirk and just enough snark to make Gideon want to shake him. Gideon told himself to calm down and focus, even though there was no money at stake. The satisfaction of winning over Luke would be compensation enough. Besides, he would never live it down if Luke won. James would be cool about winning, but Luke was never one to take the high moral ground. In any case, maybe a break was what he needed. He had been studying reports all day as they came in. He still didn't understand why Eden had been targeted. He himself had just found out about her!

Fifteen minutes later, Gideon willed his leg not to bounce. He held an ace of spades. As he waited to see what card James would put down, strands of Imperial March filled the air. Conversation paused, and both groups of men sat in suspended animation for a moment until Gideon retrieved his phone from his side pants pocket.

"Father?" he queried. The ringtone was set for his father's number, but often it was his father's assistant, Joseph Park, checking to make sure he was available first.

"Are you secure?" his father asked.

"Let me go to the back of the plane," Gideon replied. There was a more private area in the back of the plane equipped with all the tech a king might need to do business while in flight. Walking back, Gideon noticed that Eden had finally turned from looking out the window. She looked at him now with a totally expressionless face.

"Excuse me," he said in English, his glance taking in both Eden and Nurse Summers. "Do you mind sitting up front for a few minutes?" The room in the back was private but not completely soundproof. He would feel more comfortable if there were less of a chance of being overheard.

"Yes, Your Highness," Nurse Summers said as she bounced right up, bringing a startled Eden with her.

As Eden moved to the aisle, Gideon could see that her nails had dug deep grooves into her upper arm. Frowning, he slid into the back room.

"Gideon are you there?" his father asked.

Gideon realized he had missed the question. "I'm sorry, sir. What was the question?"

"Who was that?" his father asked, his tone suspicious. "That didn't sound like an American accent."

"She is Eden's nurse," Gideon replied as he closed the door to the room. "It was all in my report." He didn't add that he had sent the report right before he boarded the plane.

"You're bringing an unknown person back to the island?"

Pressing two fingers on the furrowed space between his eyebrows, Gideon leaned against the door. "I thought it was best under the circumstances."

"It's done now," his father said, his tone indicating he would have done things differently. "We'll switch her out with someone more appropriate once you return to the island."

"Sounds good," Gideon replied as he began pacing the cramped confines of the small space, wondering when his father would get to the point.

"I've directed the pilot to fly into the military base instead of the one near the palace."

Gideon stopped pacing. "Why? Did you find something out? Was it . . ." He let the question hang unfinished, not wanting to name aloud his father's chief of staff.

"Yes," his father replied, his tone curt. "He thought once he got Segenam's father out the way, he would be the next head of Sector 16."

"But why keep Eden in the UK?" Gideon asked as he tried to figure out that puzzle. "She was supposed to continue on to the island."

"Pure greed," his father replied, disgust evident in his voice. "In his defense, he did want to give Segenam's sister a chance to marry into our family, concentrating his political influence. Did I tell you he was Segenam's uncle?"

"No," Gideon replied, shocked. "How did we miss that?"

Upon his recent return to the island after two years in the military, Gideon had been sent to the temple to decompress before coming home. Instead, he'd inadvertently exposed a sex trafficking ring in which one of the other guest brothers, Segenam, was heavily involved.

Gideon's stay at the temple had ended with a road chase, an EMP blast, and a dead Segenam. The dead man belonged to Sector 16, which was led by the deceased's father. To show his displeasure, the king had ordered that no royal grants be given to the island's most prosperous sector for a year. Gideon had supposed that his father's chief of staff, as a member of Sector 16, would try to replace Segenam's father as head of the sector. He had no idea that the chief was related to Segenam.

"He was a son through a mistress, so the family relationship wasn't close," his father said.

"But wouldn't that info have shown up in his initial background screening?" Gideon asked with a perplexed frown. On the island, the stigma against single mothers had lessened, but it still existed. He figured in prior decades—he was not quite sure about the Chief of Staff's age—the stigma would have been even stronger.

"His mother was described as widowed," his father replied.

"Did he lie?" Gideon asked, aghast that someone would dare lie on their application to serve the royal family and appalled that the lie hadn't been caught until now.

"It was technically true," his father admitted. "When his mother turned up pregnant, they married her to Segenam's father's great-uncle. He had only months to live."

"Ah, I understand," Gideon said, leaning against the office door, his free hand in his pocket. "But how does this all connect to Eden? I can't imagine our Chief is related to her?"

"Former Chief," his father corrected. "He didn't want Eden to come to the island, but when he found out he could sell her to an English buyer, that's when he made the arrangements for her to be diverted."

"What was the original plan?" Gideon asked, though he feared he knew the answer.

"Eden's death," his father replied with a long sigh.

"Are you all right?" Gideon asked.

"It's most disheartening," his father explained, "to reconcile that the man I trusted the most with the island's affairs—outside of you and Gabe—could do something of this nature."

"Is it not much different than what we're doing?" Gideon said before he thought.

"Excuse me?" his father said, his voice incredulous. "In no way am I similar to former Chief Saduj Sims in that regard." This last bit was almost shouted.

"I'm extremely sorry, sir," Gideon replied, subconsciously straightening his spine. "I didn't mean to offend."

"Well, you did," his father replied brusquely. "If you didn't mean to offend, what did you mean?"

"Well, while we're not selling Eden for sex or planning her death, we are moving her around like a chessboard piece." Remembering the self-made marks on Eden's arm, Gideon said, "It's stressful for her."

"Then make it less stressful for her," the king replied.

"Yes, sir," Gideon replied, rolling his eyes before taking a deep breath and slowly exhaling.

"I've fired him, obviously," his father said, resuming discussion about his former Chief of Staff Saduj Sims.

"What, you didn't execute him?" Gideon replied and then winced. He had been in the military too long. It was true, though, that his father didn't hesitate to order executions.

"The situation is too sensitive," his father said. "The official story is that he resigned due to the stress of the job."

"That leaves him free to . . ." Gideon began as he moved in a small circle, his mind ruminating on all the ways the former Chief could cause problems.

"Your brother is handling things," his father said. "That's not why I called. There is worse news."

"What—" Gideon said, before his body jerked suddenly with the movement of the plane. "What is it?"

"What's wrong?" his father demanded.

"Nothing," Gideon replied as he pulled up a window shade. "Just plane turbulence." Seeing the seat belt sign flashing, he sat in one of two seats in the back room. "What is this worse news? Is it Ya Ya?" Gideon and his brother called their grandmother Ya Ya, a derivative somewhat of her name, Priya.

"Angel escaped," his father said.

Two simple words, but they brutally and mercilessly pummeled Gideon. His stomach involuntarily tightened, and he hunched his shoulders forward defensively. Frustrated by his own reaction, he fisted his free hand and knocked it repeatedly against his forehead before he made himself stop.

"How?" he finally managed to croak out as he clenched his leg painfully. "Saduj?"

"No," his father replied. "I thought so too at first, but the real story is complicated."

"I'm stuck on this plane for hours," Gideon replied, his voice closer to its normal octave.

"She escaped over a year ago," his father began.

"What! No way! How . . ." Gideon started to jump up, but the seat belt held him back.

"Stop talking and listen!" his father commanded.

Gideon took a deep breath before responding, "I'm listening."

"Thank you," his father replied archly. "As you know, two years ago, I ordered Angel's execution. All thirty-five members of the terrorist group Seven were to be executed. Fortunately for Angel, her father, Minister Kang, volunteered to die in her place. She still was to spend life in prison, which was less than she deserved, as you well know."

Gideon remained silent. He knew Angel was a treasonous traitor, but the thought of her dying had grieved him. He had tentatively broached the concept of mercy, but his father's anger had been great and not appeasable. He hadn't counted on Angel's father standing in for her execution.

Gideon's father harrumphed at this lack of response. "In any case, all reports showed that she was a model prisoner, doing what she was told until about fifteen months ago when it looked like she died from a brain aneurysm."

"She died?" Gideon gasped out.

"Not really," his father replied. "Hold on, your mother's calling me."

The turbulence around the plane had settled, but inside Gideon, chaos reigned. When the seat belt sign turned off, he quickly untethered himself but remained seated, the fingers of his free hand drumming on his father's desk and his knee jerking up and down.

"I'm back," his father finally said. "Where were we?"

"Angel having an aneurysm but not really," Gideon replied.

"Oh yes," his father said. "There was a visiting nurse at the prison. She was placed by an agency that gives work to foreigners who wanted to travel. Her contract at the prison medical clinic was for one year. A few weeks ago, the employment agency that placed the nurse called the medical clinic to increase the hourly rate they charged for her place-ment, only to be told that the nurse had resigned months ago. Long story short—because I have to get on another call soon—the woman had just disappeared."

"How is that possible?" Gideon interjected. *What did that have to do with Angel?*

"As much as I hate her twisted soul, Angel is a quick thinker," his father replied with a sound halfway between a huff and a sigh.

"She was always the smartest of the three of us," Gideon said as guilt flooded through him. Would Angel have introduced the *Denique Sperma* virus to his brother with him as an unwitting accomplice if he hadn't turned their childhood friendship into something sordid? He had used her genuine feelings to satisfy his own lust, knowing he didn't care for her the way she cared for him.

"Well, in this case," his father continued, "she used her wits when an opportunity presented itself. She and the nurse were the same build. It happened that Angel was with one other prisoner in the recreational room with only two guards. The guards moved away from their station due to an altercation between other prisoners in another area. The video feed shows the other prisoner had fallen asleep. Angel was the only person who saw the nurse fall."

"Ugh," Gideon growled out. "I think I see where this is going."

"Yes," his father said. "Angel dragged the nurse into the washroom located conveniently nearby and changed uniforms. She put her hair in a knot like the nurse's and put on her earrings. Everyone assumed the nurse was Angel and recorded her death."

"What? The nurse died?" Did Angel . . ." Gideon started.

"Inconclusive," his father responded. "The nurse was alive when Angel dragged her into the washroom. We can see this from the video. However, she was dead when the guards found her later."

"But no one told me," Gideon burst out.

"I told them not to tell you," the king said firmly. "I wasn't sure you were strong enough to hear the news then."

After an awkward silence, Gideon asked, "But how did no one notice that the nurse didn't look the same?"

"It was her first day in that area and the regular guards were out, so they used guards from the men's prison," his father replied. "We also discovered that Angel went through the necessary doors only when someone else was present, so she didn't have to use her fingerprint to pass through. She resigned the same day as the real nurse died."

"But the money?" Gideon asked. "Who got the nurse's paycheck?"

"I thought the same," his father said, his tone approving. "If we could follow the money, we'd catch Angel, but it is still sitting in the nurse's bank account. We are investigating why someone who did not show up to work was still getting paid."

"Island bureaucracy at its finest," Gideon replied, feeling a momentary pang for whoever was going to lose their job over the payments, before turning to the topic foremost in his mind. "But she's still missing?"

"Hold on," his father replied before quickly coming back to the phone. "I'm sorry, Gide. I do have to go now. But I need you to be extremely careful with Eden. My agent at her school used hidden cameras and there was a facial recognition hit for Angel at the Jasmine House at the school. It can't be a coincidence that the girls from that house started the fire that drove Eden from the Jade Vine House. I asked our agent to get her out as quickly as possible."

"I'll protect Eden," Gideon assured his father.

"I expected as much," his father said.

Upon exiting the small room, Gideon frowned when he couldn't see Eden. The card games were still going on. Eden's nurse was sitting next to the three men playing cards, a look of avid interest on her face, her notepad held loosely in her hand.

Expecting to see Eden sleeping, Gideon checked the seats as he walked back toward the front of the plane. Just as he reached Luke and James, he heard the unmistakable sound of a toilet flushing from the back of the plane. Gideon's own face flushed as he remembered the claustrophobia-inducing washroom tucked in the corner of the back office. You could enter the washroom from inside the office or via the larger plane area. He never considered that someone would use that washroom when there were two larger ones up front. Had she heard the conversation with his father?

Gideon turned back around.

"What, you thought she jumped off the plane?" Luke said.

While Gideon's impolite finger itched to issue a visual directive to Luke, he let his better nature prevail and kept walking back.

"I can assist her, sir," Nurse Summers said, suddenly remembering her job.

Turning sideways so he could see the nurse, Gideon said, "No need. I would like to talk with Eden for a moment."

The nurse looked uncertain at his response, but Gideon heard the washroom door open and returned his focus to Eden. Instead of hugging herself tightly, she held on to one of the seats, her gaze down, her face paler than before.

"Shall we talk?" he asked.

Eden straightened herself, clasping her hands in front of her while taking a deep breath, before saying in a bright voice. "Yes, sir, that would be delightful."

Her tone and demeanor were so out of sync with the Eden he'd seen up to then that Gideon barked out a laugh. "Good show."

Eden's slightly round cheeks bloomed rosy under her tawny complexion, and she wrapped her arms around herself again. Looking at the red scratch marks on her arms once more, Gideon frowned as he realized her nails had broken through her skin in a few places.

"You're not dressed suitably," he said.

"I'm sorry, sir," she whispered almost inaudibly as she looked down, her nails still digging.

"No," he replied, "I'm sorry. I assumed the nurse would make sure you had a sweater for the plane. One of her job duties was obtaining a few sets of clothes for you." He turned to call the nurse over.

"Sir," she said more firmly than before. "It's not the nurse's fault. The sweater scratched my skin, so I took it off. I preferred the blanket." She tilted her head to the blanket lying haphazardly on the seat she had initially sat in.

"Then use it," he said as he leaned over to get the blanket. He moved to put it around her, but at her step back, Gideon instead held it out to her. After she had wrapped the blanket around her, Gideon indicated that she should sit. He sat on the seat directly across from her, on the other side of the aisle. He pushed the chair arm up so he could sit sideways leaning toward her.

"Do my sleeves need to be longer for the . . . the island?" she stammered out.

Gideon's forehead furrowed as he tried to decipher her meaning. His confusion must have shown on his face.

"I mean, is my attire considered immodest?" Eden asked, her cheeks red again. She didn't look at him as she spoke.

Now that he understood, Gideon laughed. "No, I've seen women in much less on the island."

Her head popped up at that comment, her startled gaze meeting his amused one.

Realizing what he had said, Gideon grimaced and slapped his forehead with his hand. "My apologies again," he said. "The dress code on the island is probably more focused on designer labels than what's covered. Your jeans and T-shirt are fine."

She nodded before looking down again, her cheeks still slightly pink. Studying her now, he was struck anew by how much she resembled the knitting woman from his dreams. Periodically, he would dream of a woman in a pink dress, with riotous dark-gold curls covering her back. In his dreams, she would be knitting a red scarf. Unfortunately, the dream was sometimes a harbinger of bad things to come, like his brother's wife losing their child during her first pregnancy.

When he had flown out to rescue Eden, he had been provided with a picture of her. He had thought then that she was the girl from his dreams. But Eden was clearly younger than the woman in his dreams. It was his turn to look away as he remembered Eden telling him she was sixteen. He had felt like a dirty old man holding her hand then, despite knowing his parents intended for them to eventually marry.

"Is something the matter?" Eden asked, her hands fidgeting with the blanket around her.

Disturbed by her obvious discomfort, Gideon asked, "Do you like to knit?"

Eden's eyes widened as she stared at him before shaking her head. "I can't get the hang of two needles. I prefer to crochet." Her hands remained blessedly still for once.

"What's your favorite color when you crochet?" he asked, cringing inwardly at the inanity of the question, driven more by curiosity than a desire to put her at ease.

"I love blues and greens?" she answered with a question in her voice and a slight tilt of her head.

"Not reds or pinks?" he asked, figuring in for a penny, in for a pound.

She scrunched up her nose. "No."

Ignoring his urge to laugh at her obvious distaste, Gideon asked, "Do you have an older sister?"

"No," she replied, her hands beginning to fidget with the blanket again. "Were you expecting someone else?"

If he told her he was comparing her to a woman he had only met in his dreams, Gideon figured she would look at him in horrified dismay.

"No," he said lightly, leaning back. "Sorry to sound like an inquisition."

She shrugged one shoulder, her expression remaining puzzled before turning away to look out the plane window.

Feeling like he had screwed things up, Gideon searched for something to say.

"You seemed bothered earlier?" Eden asked, surprising him.

"I'm concerned about the attacks on you in the UK," he said, looking away from her, wondering if he should explain about Saduj and Angel.

"Is that why we left that country?" Eden asked. "I will be safer on the island?"

Deciding to play it safe, Gideon responded, "The family has enemies, just like any other family in our position. Since you'll be our ward, people may try to come after you, but you'll be protected."

"Thank you," she said with a tight smile, but her hands were fidgeting again. He heard the unspoken doubt, and he couldn't blame her. She had been attacked twice within the span of a few days. He wondered why she had chosen to leave with him. Dr. Brown had given her the option to stay and explore options for school in the UK. He had frowned at the intensity of the doctor's pitch, worried that Eden might want to stay in the UK and that he'd have to override her wishes and get her to the island. He winced as he remembered the doctor's words.

"I have a moral imperative to let her know she has options and choices," the doctor implored. "She's not a thing to be owned just because . . ."

"I want to go," Eden had interrupted.

The doctor's face fell, and her eyes became teary. Eden reached for her as though to comfort her, but the doctor took Eden's hand instead, holding it between her own hands.

"I know Nurse Summers will be with you on the plane, but once you get to the island, you need to see a doctor as soon as possible," she said.

At Eden's nod, she hugged the girl tightly and wrote all of her contact numbers on the discharge paperwork which she gave directly to Eden, rudely ignoring Gideon. He had let the insult stand as he understood she was trying to make sure Eden was safe.

At the hospital, he had been bothered by Emma's cavalier questioning of Eden. He never would have thought Emma would end up as a diplomatic liaison. She had all the subtlety of a bull in a porcelain shop. At least his parents had ensured the guardianship paperwork was thorough so there would be no questions asked about her leaving with him.

"Why did you come with me instead of staying with Dr. Brown?" he asked, crossing his arms across his chest.

"'Bad Boy Royals,'" Eden said without hesitation.

"What?" he said uncertainly.

"I watched 'Bad Boy Royals'; that's why I decided to come with you."

Gideon scratched his head. "You think I'm a bad boy royal?"

"No," Eden said, waving her hand as though trying to think of something. "Umm, at home, the media is different—just focused on government statements."

"At home, you mean Saved America?" Gideon asked.

Eden nodded. "But at the hospital, I saw there were all types of shows on the TV. I ended up watching a show with two hosts, Jack and Gwen? They were talking about Princess Charlotte?"

Gideon guffawed before finally composing himself. He asked, "You were watching *The Glitter Tattle*?" He pressed a button on the screen on the back of the chair in front of him. At his oral command, a picture of the show's blond hosts came up.

"Is this it?" Gideon motioned for Eden to lean over to see.

"Yes!" Eden said after leaning far over to look. "You found it."

"Eden, do you want a snack?" Nurse Summers had joined them, looking over Eden carefully.

So quickly he almost missed it, Gideon saw Eden subtly roll her eyes. "I'm fine," she said right before her stomach rumbled.

"It's a good idea," Gideon said, pressing the button for the flight attendants. The two flight attendants tended to stay in the background because they knew that he, like his father, hated to be hovered over. Now, he winced as he realized the other passengers may have been hungry but were waiting for him to ask for food to be served.

After the flight attendants had brought everyone their orders, Nurse Summers sat with Eden while they both ate chocolate chip cookies and drank milk.

"It's so nice when sugar's available," he overheard Eden say. He thought it was odd, but he wanted to see the episode to figure out why she came with him instead of Dr. Brown.

Two blond hosts, one male and one female, Jack and Gwen, sat at a long desk and promised "never-seen-before footage." The words "Bad Boy Royals" were posted in crooked letters at the bottom of the screen.

"Exciting news for our royal watchers!" the female announcer began with her eyes wide and a breathless voice. "Princess Charlotte and her husband, Bartholomew, the Duke of Rivergold, had a bouncing baby boy named Prince Gavin."

"That's right, Gwen," the male announcer replied. "Prince Gavin is the second in line to the throne, right behind his mother, Princess Charlotte."

"Do you think his son's birth will make the Duke of Rivergold settle down?" Gwen asked, a serious look on her face. In the next ten minutes, Gideon learned that the duke had no fewer than seven previous girl-friends at his wedding to the princess. Gideon had only known about four—or was it five? It didn't really matter. The two hosts indicated that there was rampant speculation that the princess had gotten knocked up before the wedding.

"Are you daft?" Gideon asked the hosts. The princess's baby was born eleven months after her wedding.

"What?" He heard Eden say, her tone shocked.

"Sorry," he said. "Bad habit I have of yelling at the screen."

At this point, Nurse Summers excused herself, holding up her chocolate-smeared hands and a dirty napkin as her explanation. Not mentioning that there were wipes available, Gideon sat silently as she got up to wash her hands.

Back on *The Glitter Tattle*, he watched another ten minutes of picture after picture of the duke with various ex-girlfriends, complete with interviews as the same women either declared him a saint or an unfeeling beast who toyed with their emotions. Gideon felt a little bad for Princess Charlotte. The whole point of the episode seemed to be to humiliate her.

Sick of watching and not understanding the connection with Eden agreeing to come to Seahorse Island, Gideon moved to turn off the screen, but then it filled with a larger-than-life image of the princess. She was undeniably beautiful, her small elfin face framed by dark hair cut at her jaw. But her eyes made him pause. They were large and gray and filled with sadness. In the background, the show's co-host mentioned that the princess was one for doing good works but that the duke wanted her to be more careful and not to be so touchy-feely.

"Is it appropriate," Gwen asked, "for a future queen to be so familiar with her subjects?" Her pursed mouth left no doubt that Gwen disapproved of the princess's familiarity. The screen changed to show a video of the pregnant princess awkwardly bending down to talk with homeless youth sitting outside a library.

"She might want to show more respect for her security team," the male host said, equally as scandalized as his co-host. "This was an impromptu stop."

This damning statement was followed by ominous-sounding music and video footage of young people whose desperate devil-may-care grins were at odds with their rail-thin bodies and not-quite-clean physical appearances. They were all standing in line for an on-the-job training opportunity that paid even during training.

The worst images were the dejected faces of all the youth turned away after a certain number of applicants was reached. One young woman sat down in the middle of the sidewalk and covered her face with her hands. A little girl, still a toddler, leaned against the young woman to hug her.

Sighing, Gideon turned the screen off. His mind churned as he tried to think of the implications of the show for Eden. Turning his head, he saw that she was facing him, but her gaze was down.

"If I stayed," she began haltingly before raising her own tear-filled eyes to his. "If I stayed there in the UK, that could be me."

Gideon began to protest, but she cut him off. "Consider it. I'm from Saved America, which everyone in the UK thinks is backward. What if I couldn't get a job?"

"Don't wor—" Gideon began.

"That show made me see how dependent I am on others," Eden explained. "If I could continue with schooling, I should be able to support myself after . . ." Her gaze looked toward the front of the plane before continuing, ". . . after everything."

With a wry look on her face, she continued. "It seems wrong that I'm sitting here enjoying cookies and milk like a little kid while other people my age are struggling to eat."

Gideon moved quickly into the aisle and knelt by the side of her seat. "Don't apologize for enjoying a little bit of happiness," he commanded. "You've been through horrible events over the last few days. You deserve good things." He looked around for a napkin or something for Eden to wipe her face, which had a little smear of chocolate.

"And she doesn't," came the unexpectedly sharp response from Eden. "She deserves the life she is living?" Eden gestured toward the blank screen, but Gideon thought he understood to whom she referred.

God, help me, Gideon thought to himself as he looked at Eden. *I'm not really sure how to answer her question.*

In the silence that stretched between them, Eden's expression turned contrite, and she bit her bottom lip before saying, "I'm sorry, sir."

"No," Gideon said, handing her his own napkin. "Don't apologize. Your point is valid. I just don't have a good answer."

Eden wiped her fingers instead of her face. "I guess you can't be both a prince and a philosopher."

"*Au contraire*, Eden," Gideon said with a smile, pleased she was able to find humor despite her worries. "My philosophy is that life is frequently hard, but we're given moments of happiness as gifts. Some of us are given more gifts than others, and some of us just don't realize when happiness is there for the taking, like that cookie still on your plate."

Eden shook her head, but she smiled slightly.

"Eden," Gideon said as he held out his hand to her.

Wide-eyed, Eden took it.

"I promise to protect you," Gideon said earnestly, wanting her to believe it.

Eden just stared at him and then looked down. "I heard you say the same on the phone."

Gideon thought back. "You heard that?" he asked, wondering how much of his conversation with his father she had heard.

"Only that part," she replied, distressed eyes rising to lock on his before continuing in a rush. "I didn't want to pass everyone at the front, so I went to the back, but then I remembered you wanted privacy—"

"It's fine," Gideon interjected, relieved she had not heard much. "I did tell my father I would protect you, and now I'm telling you the same."

Eden nodded, but Gideon felt awkward as he realized the other passengers were either overtly or discreetly observing his interaction with Eden.

A little embarrassed, he moved to stand up and began to release her hand, but Eden tightened her grip.

She looked up at him and spoke in a rush, "I want to find out what happened to my family and friends?"

"Make a list of everyone, and I will get started on it immediately," he said, hoping his father wouldn't object.

She nodded in response.

Gideon started to let go of her hand again, but again she tightened her hold ever so slightly. She started talking, but her voice was so low he couldn't hear her.

"I can't hear you," he said as he kneeled again and leaned closer.

"If we part ways in seven years, will that really be okay?"

"It will really be okay; I promise," he said with a wide smile.

"Thank you," she whispered with a tremulous smile of her own.

He swore to himself that it was just turbulence that made his stomach drop.

3

EDEN, FORTY-SOMETHING DAYS

"*E*den, we should probably get going if you want to see the twins," Nurse Summers said, looking at her watch phone.

We were on our way to the palace nursery, but my attention had been caught as usual by the view. On the main level, the floor extended further out from the mountain than on the more recessed upper levels. But instead of being fronted by the palace's ubiquitous stone walls, the main level was composed of glass windows that went up from the floor to the ceiling, melding into a slanted skylight above, giving me a panoramic view of the island.

On my first visit to the main level, I had gawked in astonishment at the island's riotous colors. Grasses swayed in a monochromatic ripple of purple, only to be interrupted by flowers dressed in a dizzying array of colors. Single words were inadequate to describe them. One flower was the deep dark blue of the unfathomable depths of the sea, while another was the pale blue of a bitterly cold winter morning. Magenta, in all its various pigment variations, was a popular color. The stalks were often the same color as the flowers they supported. The petals were arranged into perfectly shaped delicate balls until enticed by the sun to slowly open, revealing even smaller balls that would open as well and release a small amount of pleasant fragrance. If the inner petals were a different color than the outer petals, it was considered an omen of good fortune.

This awe-inspiring view went on for miles on a slight slope, until there was a sharp cliff and then the rest of the island came into view. Sighing, I turned my head from the window reluctantly. It was a cloudy day anyway.

"I guess I'm ready," I said.

"Don't sound so excited," Nurse Summers said with an understanding smile.

"I wish—" I said before jumping as thunder reverberated against the glass window. Nurse Summers did the same, and we both laughed at the sight of heavy rain sliding down the glass.

I guess we were both on edge, trying to adjust to the rhythm and customs of semi-royal life. Besides, I was feeling caged-in more and more, no matter how I tried to rationalize my new reality. Even now with the rain flowing like a river, if given the chance, I would have run outside. I imagined the view from the palace windows would always entice me, no matter the weather. With the rain, the view was softly distorted, like an impressionist painting. I knew some would say my life was like a painting, statically beautiful. Unfortunately, I felt as though I had exchanged one prison for another.

I'd never left the palace since I'd entered it six weeks before. Gideon had said he would protect me, but his family seemed to care more about not being embarrassed by me. According to Gideon's mother, Queen Jasmine, my Sorean language skills were as lacking as my knowledge of the culture.

That didn't make me feel too horrible, because, after all, it was true. I had only recently started learning the language and culture. It wasn't, however, like I couldn't learn a language. I spoke both classroom French and Spanish fluently. I winced, though, when I remembered the tutor's assessment of my math and science skills.

"While she has the ability to think mathematically," the tutor had said, "it's clear no attempt was made to learn anything beyond fifth-grade math, and she has absolutely no concept of science."

Thus, three weeks ago, Queen Jasmine had sat me down after breakfast and explained that I would spend my mornings improving my knowledge of math and science, my afternoons learning the Sorean culture and language, my early evening hours doing martial arts for exercise, and my after-dinner hours training for what was expected of me as a "ward" of the royal family. The kitchen staff would not send up anything that hadn't been approved by the nutritionist on staff. I guess the food part was the result of the countless medical examinations to which I was subjected.

As I wondered whether to ask about my medical results, the queen leaned forward with her elbows on her desk. "Eden," she said with a tight smile, "you must do your very best, yes?"

Or else what? I questioned silently as I nodded and smiled back at her, perched on the edge of an uncomfortable chair in front of her desk.

As she had encouraged, I tried my best, and so far, I hadn't broken down and spiraled so deep into my emotions that I couldn't climb out, something that had happened at the Joseph Hyde School for Exceptional Girls. It was, nonetheless, a bit unnerving being the focus of such unequivocal and undivided attention. Since that day in her office, I had spent more and more of my small slivers of free time looking out windows and wondering when I would get to explore the island.

Oh, no one came out explicitly and said, "Eden, you will be locked in this palace forever." But I was deemed not quite ready to represent the Royal Family Li. In the Bible, forty days and nights were like some sort of limit. I was now on the forty-second day on the island and felt absolutely stir-crazy, but I had to hide exactly how stir-crazy I was in order to be permitted outside.

I knew from the view and from my lessons what was on the island, but I wanted to bike around the parks near the Golden Bowl Plaza, walk in the farm fields, feel the texture of the island's exotic plants, visit the Temple, shop in the little boutique stores, and maybe even stay overnight at the Merman Hotel.

"Are you kissing the window?" Nurse Summers asked, a hint of amusement in her voice.

I had fogged the window with my breath, standing even closer to it than before. Flushing, I used my hand to clear away the fog and began walking with Nurse Summers.

"What were you staring at so hard?" she asked, walking a little more quickly than usual.

"Everything," I replied, my own pace increasing as well.

At her puzzled glance, I floundered for something safe to say. I liked Nurse Summers, but I didn't know how many of our conversations were reported to my new family. "I really want to visit the library," I blurted out.

"Oh, you have to see it," she replied, moving her hands around as she talked. "It's absolutely gorgeous."

I stopped and looked at her. "You've seen it?" I asked, trying but failing to keep the jealousy out of my voice.

"Yes," she replied, a worried frown on her face. "It was on my day off. They have tours for foreigners, so I went to one for English speakers."

"That's nice," I said unconvincingly and turned away. I knew it was petty, but it stung that she had been allowed to go out and I hadn't.

"Eden," she said, touching my arm lightly so that I turned and faced her.

"I know," she began, "that the family is considering what will be your first public event. You will be ready. Just be patient."

"I'm tired of being patient. I just want to go to the library," I complained, letting my shoulder slump.

Nurse Summers sighed, stepping closer and wrapping me in a warm hug.

I stiffened slightly before I relaxed. I wasn't used to being hugged. Awkwardly, I patted her back.

"Too much?" she asked as she pulled back.

"Yes," I replied, "very western culture."

As I was American and from the west side of the globe, we both tittered at my little joke. And just like that, the air cleared between us.

"Okay," she said, but she drew out the word like she was humoring me. "I never realized you had a thing for libraries." She motioned for me to proceed. "The family definitely needs to let you out more, but for now let's go visit the babies."

As we walked, I pondered her comment. I guess I did have a thing for libraries, but it was more than just books. Back home in Sunny City, New Jersey, the library was in a square, utilitarian two-story building. But I always entered it with anticipation thrumming through me. I loved the discovery of a good book.

Mrs. Walsh, the librarian, would frequently put books to the side just for me. Even more fun were the library patrons. Being homeschooled at the time, my group of friends was limited to who my parents thought appropriate. But at the library, I saw all sorts of people, even though everyone adhered to the standards set by the morality inspectors.

Now that my feelings for my childhood hometown were more attenuated, I could also remember more clearly the cracked sidewalks, the window that leaked in the common room so that no books could be put along that particular wall, and the odd book where a page or two would be torn in half or missing, always at the most critical part.

When I was taken to the Joseph Hyde School for Exceptional Girls, I thought the library might be my refuge, but I will say no more other than I was sadly disappointed. I didn't think I would be let down by the library at Seahorse Island. It sat above the island's culture building in the shape of a globe, covered in blue glass.

Of course, the palace had its own library and a staff member to download approved books for me. But the palace library wouldn't give me unfettered access to the net where I could try to find out information on my father and my friends. I could possibly even find out where my mother was buried. On the plane, Gideon had said he would help me search, but he hadn't said anything since I had come to the island.

Longing to know all that had been kept from me, I said a quick prayer for patience, something I did multiple times a day.

"We can spend fifteen minutes at the nursery before we have to go to breakfast," Nurse Summers said, interrupting my thoughts. From the way she twisted her lips, something she did when concentrating, I knew she was going through my schedule in her head.

With a sigh, I said, "You know, when I begged Gideon to keep you on, I didn't know you would turn into Mrs. Wright, version two."

"Oh, my apologies, Your Highness," Nurse Summers said with false sweetness. "If you prefer, I can get Mrs. Wright, who has been serving your honored family since 1536." She looked at me with a smirk.

"B.C. or A.D.?" I quipped back and we both started giggling.

Unfortunately, our laughter was cut short by the appearance of the said Mrs. Wright, who seemed to come out of nowhere; she moved so quietly, even on the towering heels she seemed to prefer. She stood with her hands clasped and gave us a slight head nod. She straightened abruptly, as though she remembered something, and stared at Nurse Summers with a hint of irritation before her face resumed its usual expressionless pose.

"I have been honored to serve this family for only twenty-seven years," Mrs. Wright began in her usual pedantic, censorious tone. With a regretful look at her wrist, she queried, "You still are not familiar with the palace? The family dining room is in the opposite direction." She gave me a grim smile, using a hand to point us in the right direction.

"Actually," I replied with a fake smile, "we're going to peek in on the twins before eating breakfast." With a regretful look at my own wrist, I said, "We only have a few moments. Please excuse us."

With a reluctant look, Mrs. Wright moved to the side.

Once we had passed her, Nurse Summers and I moved quickly to the nursery, but with a slight hand on my shoulder, the nurse stopped me just before we reached the door. I could hear one of the twins babbling.

"What is it?" I asked with an impatient glance at the door.

"What was the deal with Mrs. Wright?" she asked, but then Princess Lily stepped out of the room.

"Eden!" she exclaimed in Sorean. "Come in! The girls are rolling all over the place."

I was pleased to have understood her. Six weeks of being forced to speak the language continually made me more proficient. My pleasure was short-lived when I made a quick bow to her, which made me realize that perhaps I should have bowed to Mrs. Wright? I couldn't seem to get a handle on the bowing protocol. Too many rules and exceptions to the same rules. I was to bow to folks older than me but not to family. As a ward of the royal family, I was considered family and shouldn't bow within the family. But since the family was the royal family and not just any family, I had to do a slight bow to family members older than me when in the presence of non-royals. With a sigh, I pushed those thoughts aside and played with the twins.

"Good job, Addie!" I clapped my hands lightly together in applause as she turned over onto her back. I spoke in English as I could understand more of Sorean than I could say.

She smiled back at me, her whole body wiggling in happiness. I poked her little belly, which set her to squealing.

"I love your nickname for her!" Lily exclaimed as she sat on the floor on the opposite side of Aditya, or Addie as I called her. Amara lay right beside Lily and looked up at her mother's voice before trying to stick her foot in her mouth.

Lily shook her head, saying, "Well, aren't we a little Einstein today!"

"I think that's normal for babies," Nurse Summers said with a smile.

"I know it's normal," Lily replied with an edge to her voice.

I liked Lily, but in my time on the island, I had discovered her moods could shift quite quickly, mostly for the negative. When she was in a bad mood, it was best to get away as soon as possible.

"Your daughters are absolutely perfect," I said, trying to soothe things as I stood up with Addie. She hated for visitors to stand and leave her on the floor, so I'd learned to pick her up and hand her to one of the nannies before I left.

"Well, they would have to be perfect for me to love them," Lily replied, looking at Amara without smiling, her expression grim and her face even paler than usual, almost bloodless, contrasting sharply with her glossy dark hair pulled upward into a convenient bun.

Nurse Summers and I looked at each other, stunned. Recovering, I said, "Aren't all children perfect to their parents?"

Addie started to fuss, and I rocked her from side to side to calm her.

"That's true, but not always," Nurse Summers tentatively ventured.

Lily's eyes narrowed as she looked at the nurse. "Explain," she commanded.

My watch phone beeped, letting me know that Nurse Summers and I should be on our way to the dining room, but Lily needed to be heading there as well. I bit my lower lip lightly as I hoped the nurse's explanation was brief.

"Sometimes kids are perfectly healthy and fine, but their parents can't see their worth," the nurse explained as she walked to the door, and I handed the baby off to a nanny. "Sometimes kids have health conditions that are chronic or just part of who they are, and their parents love them completely. Are you ready?" She already had one foot out the door, and I was right behind her. We both looked at Lily expectantly, but her lips were twisted in a nasty sneer. I recoiled from the disdain emanating from her.

"Must be nice to believe in such simple platitudes," she scoffed. "Maybe that's why Gideon let you stay. A stupid companion for a stupid girl."

Lily stood up, holding Amara, who chose that moment to start crying in her mother's arms. Addie looked over from the safety of the nanny's arms.

"You're holding her too tight," Nurse Summers said to Lily, her voice rising to be heard over Amara.

Lily handed a still-crying Amara to the other nanny.

I could feel my stress level rise as I realized there was no way to be on time for breakfast. I reasoned that if all three of us were late, we wouldn't be reprimanded too much.

"Do you have kids?" Lily asked snidely. "Or is child-rearing something you read about in a book?"

"I'm sorry for overstepping," Nurse Summer replied, her voice and face expressionless.

Out of the periphery of my eye, I registered movement and turned my gaze back to Lily, watching her stalk over to us but realizing her intentions too late.

"No!" I cried out as Lily raised her hand and slapped the nurse's face. The loud sound of the smack made Amara cry louder. She was nearly hysterical.

As Addie started up too, Nurse Summers, Lily, and I stood as still as statues. Nurse Summers held her cheek with both hands, her lips pressed tight together as she glared at Lily.

For her part, Lily's hand was still raised, her mouth opening and closing as if she meant to speak but kept forgetting the words.

My stomach clenched as I desperately tried to think of what to say. The two nannies avoided looking at us, concentrating on soothing the twins.

"Lily!" It was Gabriel, Lily's husband.

When Nurse Summers moved so he could come in, he walked directly to Lily and wrapped her in a hug. "Honey, tell me what's wrong."

Lily started crying like her daughters, and the noise made me want to cover my ears and scream myself. But I didn't, just stood there and absorbed the pain and sadness swirling around me.

Pain and resolve covered Gabriel's face. With Lily's face pressed into his chest, he motioned for me and Nurse Summers to leave.

As we left, I tripped at the doorway. Looking down, I saw the silver necklace Lily always wore. Its heart-shaped pendant had broken on top, so I could see half of a picture underneath. As I picked it up, the other top half came off and I saw the full picture of the baby. There was something different about the baby's face. I looked closer.

"Eden!"

Startled, I looked up.

"Let's go!" Nurse Summers commanded, yanking me up and out the door. She moved to slam the door, but at the last second, she grabbed the doorknob to stop its momentum and gently closed the door.

"I was so mad over this," she said as she pointed at her still-red cheek, "that I forgot about the babies for a second. You ready?"

We ran to the Li Family dining room, ignoring the surprised faces of those we passed. Panic shot through me at the thought of being late. The family had been so nice to me, but I suffered this underlying persistent fear that I would be kicked out of the palace with nowhere to go.

In addition to the anxiety, confusion swelled in my head, making it ache. Why was Lily so weird? What had caused the pain in Gabriel's eyes? And why was Lily carrying around a picture of another baby?

"You're late," Mrs. Wright said from her position by the dining room doors. King Edward, Queen Jasmine, Prince Gideon, his grandmother

Ya Ya, and Brother Adam were seated but it didn't appear as if anyone had started eating.

Nurse Summers executed a proper deep bow beside me as I uncomfortably hunched over, feeling my cheeks flush. But before I could mumble my apologies, Nurse Summers said, "My sincerest apologies for bringing Eden to breakfast late."

"Where are Gabriel and Lily?" the queen asked.

"They were detained in the nursery," Nurse Summers spoke, still holding her bowed position.

I stayed hunched over as well, feeling lightheaded as I smelled the lovely aroma from the table. Never a good idea to run on an empty stomach.

"Try to get Eden here on time tomorrow," the queen said with a languid wave of her hand, and then Nurse Summers and Mrs. Wright were dismissed.

I wished I could chase after Nurse Summers and join her in the staff dining area. I had stumbled upon it once and longed to be part of the easy camaraderie and joking around I'd witnessed. It still stung, however, to see how everyone stopped talking to look at me as Nurse Summers guided me out of the room. It wasn't lost on me that while she was friendly and open with me, she seemed the most carefree when she was with other staff. Her gaze and smile weren't so guarded then.

It wasn't that the royal family dining room wasn't nice. It was quite beautiful, all done up in silver and purple accents. As I sat at the large round table, I inhaled the tempting smells emanating from spiced vegetables and meats, as well as the ubiquitous rice. But I didn't feel at ease with everyone. At school, Kaitlyn would see the silver lining, and Bethany would see the clouds. With the people gathered here, I still didn't know what to expect.

With a sigh, I used my chopsticks—one more thing I had to learn— to reach for a strip of seasoned chicken, only to see everyone put their hands together for grace.

I hurriedly put my chopsticks down and did the same. I understood most of the prayer, but there was one sentence that eluded my understanding. Distracted by trying to decode it, I didn't realize the prayer was over until Gideon nudged my leg under the table. He was sitting to my left.

I reached again for the chicken, savoring the taste. I was starting to like eating for breakfast what would be dinner food back in Saved America.

"Slow down, Eden," the queen admonished. "You don't want to upset your stomach."

I nodded, embarrassed even though food rarely upset my stomach and I had only eaten one slim piece of chicken.

"Also, that nurse is as English as they come," the queen continued with a pointed look at me, "and she knows how to properly bow."

"It's all that bowing to the queen," Gideon interjected before shoveling rice into his mouth. I noticed his mother didn't correct his eating habits.

His parents laughed at his joke. While I was glad he had lightened her implied criticism, my stomach still clenched. There was no way I could eat comfortably now.

"I'm sorry; I will practice bowing," I said, mentally adding bowing to my already overflowing list of things to improve.

"You are doing well, learning everything in such a short time," Gideon said with an encouraging smile. "You will get it with time."

"Thanks," I replied, smiling back.

"What's so hard about it?" Queen Jasmine said. "You just bow." She shook her head as she pushed an errant hair strand back in place. As she did, I noticed a little grey at her temple, which answered my unspoken question about whether she dyed her hair, which she wore long and straight.

"It seems so . . ." I floundered as I realized saying what I thought might sound rude.

"Subservient, degrading, humiliating, and un-American," Gideon said, and I laughed out loud for the first time ever in the family dining room. Even his dad, the most serious man I had ever met, smiled—or at least the corners of his mouth went upward. Either he had gas or he was actually smiling.

"Gideon!" his mom admonished.

Her son shrugged and stuffed a piece of tofu into his apparently ravenous mouth.

"Why are you eating that?" his mom asked.

"I'm avoiding meat today," he replied.

As Gideon and his mother bickered over various diets, from my right Brother Adam placed another sliver of chicken on my plate.

"More meat for you and me," he said as he smiled, his voice raspy. Ya Ya smiled at me too, her long, snow-white hair pulled haphazardly into a loose bun.

As the warmth of their smiles spread through me, I felt myself relax.

"Eat, eat!" Ya Ya urged, making eating motions with her hands.

As soon as I put the meat in my mouth, both Brother Adam and Ya Ya asked, "Good?"

I gave them a thumbs-up and both started to laugh and then cough. I frowned when I heard them coughing, and even the queen and her son paused their bickering. But Brother Adam and Ya Ya patted each other on the back and the coughing subsided.

With their hands still touching each other's backs, the two exchanged a look that I could not interpret. Watching them, however, made me feel like I was interrupting something private.

I looked away, and as I reached for another strip of chicken, Queen Jasmine asked sharply, "Eden, what is that?" She pointed to a piece of Lily's necklace that had fallen over the edge of my shirtdress's chest pocket.

"Oh," I said, carefully pulling out the necklace and the piece that had broken off. "Lily dropped it."

"Why didn't you return it?" she asked, her voice laden with distrust.

I didn't need a language dictionary to understand the meaning behind her words. I sat in stunned silence, my hand still stupidly grasping Lily's necklace. But Ya Ya erupted, slamming her chopsticks down and speaking angrily to the queen too fast for me to catch everything, but I heard what I thought was the Sorean word for idiot.

The queen's face tightened, and she slid a furtive glance at the king, who carefully avoided looking at her. The queen pressed her lips together harder and furrowed her brows.

Ya Ya kept up her diatribe, pointing at me now and then. My insides froze as I remembered my outsider status. I had forgotten for a moment.

"That's enough," Brother Adam said quietly to Ya Ya, his hand gently touching her shoulder.

"You are too comfortable with my mother," the king said, his voice dripping with displeasure as he stared hard at Brother Adam.

Brother Adam removed his hand from Ya Ya's shoulder and bowed his head. "My sincere apologies, Your Highness."

"Are you serious?" Ya Ya interrupted incredulously.

Brother Adam held up his hand, silently asking for permission to continue speaking. "I intend to formally ask for your mother's hand in marriage. I will schedule time with your assistant."

Ya Ya turned to him, her eyes widening in amazement as happiness suffused her entire expression. She clasped her hands together over her heart before reaching out to take one of Brother Adam's hands into her own.

He placed his other hand on top of their joined hands as they stared at each other in wonder.

Witnessing their gnarled, wrinkled hands held by each other, I felt the loneliness within me deepen. I doubted I should ever experience such love.

A hand covered my own. Surprised, I turned to see Gideon leaning toward me. "I think this is an adults-only conversation."

I was so discomfited by the pull I felt toward him that it took a moment for his words to register. I dropped my gaze, nodding my acquiescence as I felt my face flush again. I hoped my cheeks weren't too red.

I moved to get up, but Gideon did too. I looked around, but everyone else remained sitting, not saying a word. The king looked truly stunned; his mouth was half-open and he sat frozen. Queen Jasmine sat with arms crossed, looking skeptically at Ya Ya and her beau.

Confused, I turned to Gideon. "I thought you were staying?"

"No, this is an 'adults-only' conversation, remember?" he teased as he tweaked my nose gently.

I laughed at his joke and was even more pleased when he laughed too. I'd only seen flashes of the playful side of Gideon.

We bowed quickly to the "adults" and left. As we stood just outside the dining room, I asked, "What should I do with this?" I held out Lily's necklace in the palm of my hand.

Gideon frowned at the baby picture and then sighed, his playful demeanor disappearing. "I'll give it to her later," he said, taking it carefully from my upturned palm.

He took a step but then turned back to me. "It's not something to be talked about."

I WAS RAVENOUSLY hungry after a humbling martial arts class in which I had my feet swiped out from under me no less than ten times, my back hitting the mat with humiliating thuds. *Thud, thud, thud,* and *thud.* My back twitched as I shuffled my way to my suite. I didn't have to worry about eating with the family. Everyone had royal engagements for dinner.

After arranging for the kitchen to send dinner to my room, I went to take a hot shower. The rose-and-jasmine-scented shampoo reminded me of my mother growing roses and other flowers. We would use their delicious fragrances in our soaps and shampoos.

Feeling another crying jag coming on, I willed it back, telling myself I would get to the bottom of what had happened to my family and friends. As I dried myself off, I thought perhaps it was more important to find out why I had been considered a suitable candidate for the Joseph Hyde School. Going to that school was the start of my linear life going sideways.

I knew why my parents had sent me. The lecherous Inspector Brown, the supervisor in charge of my hometown's morality inspectors, had taken too much interest in me. My Aunt Adeline helped arrange everything to appear as though I was kidnapped, keeping suspicion off my parents.

But it seemed we'd jumped right from the frying pan into the fire. My mom was dead. My father was suffering. As for me, I discovered quite quickly that the school was really a way for men to purchase suitable brides. To be a prospective bride, though, you had to meet certain criteria. I still had no idea why I made the cut.

I remembered Rosemary, who tried to sneak in as her sister, Ginger, but the school caught on immediately. I remembered the mysterious shots that everyone but me seemed to get. I remembered Rosemary's death. I sighed as I wiped away the fog on my washroom mirror and saw my teary expression.

"Not today," I mumbled to myself. Tonight, I would stay awake long enough to plan my next steps. I couldn't keep floating in the wind like a dandelion.

"You're not ready for dinner?" a voice said as a knock sounded at my washroom door. I jumped, my heart pounding, until I realized the voice belonged to Mrs. Wright.

Pure rage fired through my veins. I loved my suite, so different from the miserly room I'd had at school. The suite door opened into a spacious hangout area with an overlarge navy-blue-and-white striped sofa and a sky-blue loveseat. Two comfortable brown leather chairs flanked a spindly table on which I was afraid to put anything heavier than a light lamp. There were no windows, but the huge skylight overhead provided enough light for me and my few potted plants. On the opposite side of the door was a curved wall with three doors, one for the bedroom, one for my study, and one for the washroom. To have what had become my sanctuary invaded without invitation stirred some primal territorial feeling.

"What are you doing here?" I demanded, my voice slightly lower than a yell as I swung the door wide open with one hand and gripped the towel around me with the other hand.

"Royals don't yell," came the smug reply.

"They do when people walk into their suites uninvited and unannounced," I replied tartly, wondering what was wrong with me. I never —well, almost never—let my anger show.

"This is not your suite," she hissed as she moved closer to me, invading my personal space. "You're just a charity case."

My hands tightened on the towel I was wrapped in.

"And yet I still have more manners than you," I said, forcing my voice to be even.

Another knock sounded, this time at my suite door. The maliciousness in Mrs. Wright turned to wariness.

"Who is it?" I called.

"It's me, Gideon," came the reply.

Mrs. Wright's eyebrows shot up.

"Come in," I said, surprised as well as curious.

When Gideon stepped into the room in his black evening tux, his skin gleaming with good health, I almost gasped. Living with all girls for so long, I had forgotten what a male presence felt like. There had been my male teacher, Mr. Jack Holt, but that had been in secret and seemed so separate from the rest of my school life. Coming to the palace with more mixed company had been a readjustment. But with Gideon, I seemed more aware of him with each passing day.

He took in the scene and quickly averted his eyes as he fumbled with his collar. I'd forgotten I was wearing nothing but a towel. I flushed red as he said, "My event got canceled. Let's eat in the family dining room."

"I can join you in ten minutes," I replied. "I just need to get dressed."

"Excuse me, sir. I had planned to eat with the family's ward this evening to run through an etiquette lesson," Mrs. Wright said as she smiled up at the prince, her hands folded in front. "Shall I reschedule?" She put just enough regret into her voice that I was sure the prince would relent and let her do the lesson.

"Yes, you should reschedule," he said instead, his tone cold.

"Of course, sir," Mrs. Wright said with an apologetic bow.

Gideon closed my suite door with a decisive click.

Mrs. Wright shot me a venomous look, her features twisted as she also exited.

I slowly exhaled, releasing my clenched fists. I could see that my nails had made small indentations in my palm. I quickly got dressed and went to find Gideon.

When I entered the dining room, Gideon stood and frowned. "Don't you have anything with colors? You always wear black."

"It just seems easier," I replied before giving a small smile to the staff member who pulled out my chair. "At school, we only wore bright colors on special occasions."

"Do you miss school?" he asked, putting his napkin on his lap.

"I miss my friends, but not the school," I replied, hurriedly rushing to put my napkin on my lap as well. Six weeks out of school, and I was forgetting the most basic lessons.

"It must have been odd going to a school where the only qualifications were your genes and the ability to carry a baby to term."

"Wh-what?" I stuttered as water splashed my shaking hand. Confused, I put down the glass I was holding and grabbed another napkin to clean up the spilled water.

"Didn't you know?" he asked, his eyes widening as he leaned forward across from me. "I thought they trained you girls to be brides."

"Yes," I replied slowly, as I tried to make sense of his words. "Is it because of Eve's virus?" I asked.

"What virus?" Gideon said, a little bit of rice stuck to the corner of his mouth.

Exasperated, I said, "The virus that causes sterility and birth defects." Still bothered by the rice, I reached over and quickly flicked it off.

"Rice?" he asked, rubbing his hand over his mouth.

"It clashed with your suit," I said, smiling slightly.

He shrugged. "I can never eat comfortably at events."

"You feel more comfortable when you eat at the palace?" I asked, looking around at the opulence around me, in the room designed for only his family to dine.

"It's home to me. You aren't hungry?" he asked as he noticed me picking at my rice.

"I guess not," I said. "I'm still trying to figure out what you mean by the whole school thing and the virus?"

"Oh, yes," he replied, putting his chopsticks down. "The virus you were talking about, we call it the *Denique Sperma* virus, Latin for short sperm."

At my scrunched-up face, Gideon laughed again. "Why do you call it Eve's virus?"

"Because the virus is a punishment for women's sins."

Gideon's hand paused as he reached for the chopsticks again, his intense gaze lacking any trace of humor. "That's not true. A crazy man, Dr. Spike, created the mosquitos that carry the virus."

As he stared at me, I felt exposed and dumb. I had never questioned my country's explanation for the virus, and always felt a little guilty for wanting to go to university, something not focused on the home, marriage, or children. But it was clear from my short, sheltered time in the palace that not every place was like home. Was truth just relative based on where you were at the moment? If I forgot everything I grew up knowing, who would I be?

I looked down at the table between us, allowing my damp hair to fall forward so that it half shielded my face.

"I hope I didn't offend you?" Gideon asked, hesitantly.

I nodded without looking up or moving my hair. Something tickled at the back of my mind. The pieces still didn't fit together.

"But why would someone pay when they could just hire a surrogate?" I asked, twisting my hair around my hand.

Gideon shrugged. "It's a better status to not have to use a surrogate."

I looked up to see him eating fried tofu. His rapid chewing slowed as he saw my expression.

"That's it?" I asked, unconvinced.

"That's it," he replied with a chagrined expression. He put his chopsticks down. "I should explain better. We've only had one case of the virus on the island."

I waited for him to go on, but he winced and looked away from me.

"Are you okay?" I asked.

"Yes," he said, visibly shaking himself. "As I was saying, there has only been one case of the virus. My parents matched me with you because they feel we are a good genetic fit."

"That's why I'm here?" I asked.

"Yes," he said, his gaze not quite meeting mine.

"But, I can leave after seven years?" I asked, hoping by then I would find my dad and my friends. I then remembered a question I'd been meaning to ask. "Wait, your parents couldn't find someone on this island to marry you?"

He ran his hand over his hair as the tips of his ears reddened. "My parents had certain requirements." He stopped running his hand over his hair and looked at me, his gaze direct. "Look, I have no more desire to be matched this way than you do, so to answer your first question—yes, you can leave after seven years."

"What other options do I have?" I asked, but my heart squeezed painfully as I realized that the island would be another place from which I would have to leave everyone behind, including the person sitting across from me. The loneliness of my future stretched bleakly before me.

I looked away from Gideon, but he touched my shoulder to bring my attention back to him. I hurriedly blinked away an emerging tear before I looked up again.

"What other options do I have?" he asked, repeating my question back to me. "This deal was the best I could do. Do you want a cookie?" He held one out to me.

Heat rushed to my face at the blatant patronization. Still, my traitorous mouth watered as I smelled the buttery sweetness wafting past my nose. At least he had the good grace to look abashed.

"Sorry, E, I didn't want dinner to end on a bad note," he said as he moved to put the cookie back on the plate.

"E is not my name," I said curtly as I grabbed the cookie and bit into it savagely. The layered sweetness made me want to savor it, but I could not in front of Gideon, a situation that left me unreasonably frustrated.

"You're lucky you can get sugar on the island," I said as I took some cookies and moved them to the edge of my plate. I planned to save them for later.

He shook his head, amused as he handed me a napkin. "After the revolution, your government made up that story about the sugar cane shortage so it could make money selling the sugar to other countries."

"Did it work?" I asked, more curious than appalled. "Sugar cane only grows in a few states."

"The family of your president is in the sugar business," Gideon replied.

"But still, there must be a shortage elsewhere for the plan to work?" I asked.

"I assume so," Gideon answered with a shrug.

We each took a bite of our respective cookies while we looked at each other. In short order, no cookies were left to take back to my room.

It was only later, as my stomach grumbled at my overindulgence, that I remembered my determination to come up with a plan that night, or at least the start of one. I wanted to find out more information about my family and friends, but I had completely forgotten.

Hurrying to the washroom, I vomited all the sticky chewiness I had happily devoured such a short time before.

4

GIDEON, MAMA'S MAYBE

Gideon sat cross-legged, his long arms resting on his legs, palms up. Calming with each deep breath, he released one last long exhale before he slowly opened his eyes.

Brother Adam sat directly in front of him, mimicking his body position except for the sly grin on his face.

Feeling his peace vanish in a flood of irritation, Gideon barked, "What are you doing here?"

"I came to find peace," Brother Adam replied, his eyes innocently wide. "Same as you, brother."

Gideon mock gasped, his hand slapped to his chest. "Oh no, a secret brother." Leaning over, he whispered, "How exactly are we related?"

"We are all children of the most high God," Brother Adam replied simply, his gaze steady on Gideon.

"You would pull the God card." Gideon sighed as he stood and reached out his hand. "Again, why are you here?"

"To see what you're so stressed about," Brother Adam replied with a grunt as he made it to his feet, moving his hand to Gideon's arm.

"Who said I was stressed?" Gideon asked, one eyebrow raised.

"You're meditating," Brother Adam replied with his own raised eyebrow.

The two men looked at each other before bursting into laughter. Once they'd composed themselves, Gideon said, "Let's sit." He moved at a slower pace than usual as he walked to the studio's one bench, mindful of Brother Adam's hand still on his arm. He couldn't help, though, poking the bear.

"Are you going to stand up at the wedding, or am I going to have to walk with you then too?" he asked playfully. He was rewarded with a hard slap on the back of his head.

"Ouch!" he yelled, rubbing the offended spot. Gideon glared at the other man, who was now sitting on the bench.

"Why did you do that?" Gideon grumbled as he flopped down on the bench as well. To be truthful, he was surprised at the old man's strength.

"You were being disrespectful," Brother Adam replied with a disapproving frown. "Your Ya Ya is a wonderful, beautiful woman. The sight of her at our wedding will give me all the strength I need," he said, his frown turning into a wistful smile.

Gideon's mouth opened and closed as he stared at Brother Adam's serious face.

"Sorry," he finally said, lightly squeezing the older man's shoulder for a moment. "It's hard to picture Ya Ya getting married."

"Love is not defined by age," Brother Adam sagely replied as he looked around. "I don't think this studio was part of the original design."

"Gabriel gave it to Lily as an anniversary present," Gideon said as he looked around the spartan studio with pale-green walls and wood floors.

"What a thoughtful gift," Brother Adam murmured.

In the momentary silence, a barely-there memory surfaced for Gideon as he reconsidered Brother Adam's statement about the studio. "Wait, you were the junior architect!" he exclaimed in amazement, pointing emphatically at the other man.

At Brother Adam's puzzled face, Gideon explained, "My great uncles told me about a junior architect who was in love with Ya Ya before she married my grandfather."

"Ah! I remember Michael and Joseph well," Brother Adam said, his voice wavering slightly.

"Did you not like them?" Gideon asked, leaning forward eagerly. "Ya Ya doesn't like them either."

"Don't be such a gossip." Brother Adam sniffed disdainfully. "They just reminded me that there was no way for us to be together, not with your grandfather interested in possessing her."

"You mean marrying her?" Gideon asked with a slight frown.

"That too."

"I suppose Ya Ya made the right decision, then," Gideon said uncertainly. He knew his grandfather, the first King Li, was far from a saint, but he felt obligated not to say negative things about him.

"You think I would put her in the position of choosing?" Brother Adam replied sharply, turning his whole body away.

Uncertain of how to proceed, Gideon changed the topic. He was uncomfortable anyway, thinking about his grandmother in some sort of love triangle.

"Where's your cane?" he asked. "I usually see you with it."

The other man turned back to look at Gideon. "Silence is a virtue."

"But not as much fun," Gideon replied with an unrepentant grin.

"I'm practicing walking without the cane," Brother Adam admitted with a rueful expression. "I want to be ready on my wedding day."

Gideon struggled to keep the humor from his face as he tried to nod impassively. In desperation, he turned his head away and took a breath before turning back to Brother Adam's scowling face.

"You shouldn't laugh at your elders!" he admonished.

"I'm not laughing," Gideon said with only a trace of humor. "I think it's sweet."

Brother Adam just looked at him sideways.

"I don't think Ya Ya cares," Gideon continued with a shrug. "She knew you walked with a cane before you proposed. It's you that cares."

"I do." The elder man sighed. "You'll understand when you fall in love."

Gideon fell silent as he thought of Angel. He had not loved her. He had thought he loved her as a person; he just was not *in* love with her. Even so, he had not treated her with love, and he felt torn because he could not reconcile his sense of self with his actions toward her. Every single time he thought of Angel, he was sucked into a swirling vortex of guilt and shame. He felt a hand on his shoulder and stilled. It was only at that moment that he realized he had been bouncing his left leg in agitation.

"Do you want to talk about her?" Brother Adam asked.

Gideon shook his head and leaned forward, elbows on his knees, to place his forehead in his interlinked fingers. "I need to head out soon," he said. "What are—"

"Shhhh!" a nearby voice interrupted him. Lily, Nurse Summers, and Eden giggled as they tried to simultaneously laugh and shush each other.

"Oh!" Eden said, wide-eyed as she noticed him first.

"Aren't you supposed to be studying?" he asked her.

As Eden's face flushed with guilt, Lily put an arm around her and said, "Since lessons were canceled this morning, I thought she should get a tour of the less-used rooms in the palace."

Not fooled, Gideon said, "You're hiding from Mrs. Wright."

"That too," Lily said slyly, smiling.

Gideon realized it had been a long time since he had seen her smile. He turned to Brother Adam. "I think that's our cue to leave."

As they walked past the ladies, Gideon noticed that Eden looked different. He paused until he realized her hair was long and straight.

"Did you straighten your hair?" he asked.

"Lily did it this morning," she replied shyly, gazing up at him. "Do you like it?"

He reached out and ruffled the top of her head. "Now I do!"

He laughed as she gasped and frantically smoothed down her hair.

"Get out!" Lily commanded, pointing the way for him.

After the door closed behind them, Gideon turned to ask Brother Adam where he was going, but he found the other man staring at him as if he were trying to figure something out.

"What?" he asked.

But Brother Adam just shook his head. As they walked away, they ran into Mrs. Wright. Normally, Gideon would have nodded and moved on, but he halted so she would have to stop as well.

"Is everything all right, Mrs. Wright?" he asked politely.

"I'm trying to catch up with your family's ward, sir," she replied with a tight smile, but Gideon noticed the hardness in her eyes.

"Did you check the library?" he asked.

"Thank you, sir," she said with a slight bow before walking in the direction of the library.

He heard the studio door behind him open and made motions with his hand to stay back without turning around. He heard the click as the door closed just as Mrs. Wright turned around with a slightly puzzled look. Gideon looked back at her innocently, and she nodded deferentially before moving on more briskly.

"This morning," Brother Adam began as they continued on, "I'm learning much about you."

"I could say the same, Brother," Gideon said with a sideways glance at the older man. "How is it, seeing the place you designed?"

"I was only a junior architect back then," Brother Adam replied modestly. "But the scale is quite larger than I remember."

"Truly?" Gideon asked. "Very little has changed since my brother and I were born."

"Hmm," Brother Adam replied. "I wasn't aware that human history began when you were born. I'm going to have to contact all the libraries and museums all over the world and tell them to make the correction right away."

"Ha ha." Gideon stopped walking and glared at the other man, who paused as well.

Brother Adam sighed. "The palace is designed beautifully. Perhaps I'm just envious," he replied with a shake of his head. "When your grandfather insisted that the castle be built into the mountain, we all complained about the lack of light on the mountain side." Gesturing with his hands, Brother Adam continued. "We thought we were geniuses for coming up with the skylights in front, but having one in the center here from top to bottom really brightens the interior."

"But?" Gideon queried.

"It's double the size of the original design. This second level that we're on would have been the top level. A top layer has been added along with a lower level."

"It's a lot smaller than Buckingham Palace," Gideon replied with a frown. "Are you saying it's ostentatious?"

"Heaven help me," Brother Adam replied with an upward glance. "All palaces are ostentatious. It's the whole point of a palace."

"Then why are you annoyed?" Gideon asked with a tilt of his head.

"I am not exactly sure," Brother Adam replied as his frail shoulders slumped even further. "Back then, we were building a *kingdom*," he said with emphasis. "Now, it's already built and so established that you can't even remember it not being here. The staterooms are filled with art collected over decades."

Gideon nodded, unsure what to say. He yelped when Brother Adam unexpectedly grabbed both of his shoulders.

"Time is an enemy of us all. In the time I have left, I am going to love your grandmother with all the love I have to give."

"Please stop talking," Gideon replied as he gently removed the older man's hands. "You have my utter and complete blessing to marry my grandmother, but, please, no more confessions."

"One day you'll fall in love," Brother Adam said with a wag of his finger. "I can't wait to say I told you so."

"Well, if I wait until I'm your age to get married, you'll be long dead and hopefully only communicating with other dead people." Gideon held out his hand in the direction they were headed. "Shall we?"

Brother Adam gave a slow shake of his head. "The disrespect of young people nowadays."

THIRTY MINUTES LATER, as Gideon strode into his office suite, his assistant immediately jumped up, chattering away about phone calls and meetings.

Gideon held up a hand to stop the onslaught. "Give me an hour, and then you can come in."

"But . . ." his assistant, Timothy Plath, began as Gideon opened the door to his private office.

"Gideon," his brother Gabriel greeted him. His twin was sitting in Gideon's desk chair, making no move to get up.

"Sorry, sir," Gideon's assistant said from behind him. "He said he wanted to speak with you."

"And he couldn't wait in the—what is it?" Gideon said with a snap of his fingers. "Oh, yes! The waiting area?"

As the assistant profusely apologized and bowed, Gideon's annoyance level rose. He had a lot of things to get done. Taking Brother Adam back to his room had taken more time than expected. To make up the time, he'd skipped lunch and planned to grab an energy bar from the snack stash he kept in his office. He felt like a worm, however, when he saw the stricken countenance of Plath.

"Never mind," he muttered, aware that Plath could not tell the first in line to the throne what to do. But Gideon could. Feeling somewhat better, he closed his office door and turned to Gabriel.

"What are you doing here?" he demanded.

"I wanted to know what it felt like to be second best," his brother replied with a smug smile as he slowly unfolded his long frame from Gideon's chair.

Gideon clenched his fists at his sides to stem the sudden wrath warring within him. He and his brother had always been competitive, but they had never ventured into the cruel category. Gideon's eyes narrowed as he considered how out of character Gabriel's words were. His brother had literally welcomed him with open arms when he returned home and repeatedly told him not to worry about the past.

As he puzzled over his brother's behavior, Gideon noticed Gabriel's hand twitching and the slight redness of his eyes.

"Are you drunk?" Gideon asked, his gaze incredulous.

"I wish," Gabriel replied with a hard laugh. He pressed his finger to his forehead, his eyes closed as if in pain.

The hair stood on the back of Gideon's neck, and his own hand twitched.

"Are you sick?" he asked, wondering if there were lingering side effects from his brother's illness two years prior. The illness Gideon had caused when he gave his brother tea gifted by Angel. He barely registered the soft knocking coming from the door behind him.

Gabriel, however, tilted his head to where Plath was now poking his head in through the slightly open door, like a badger surveying the terrain.

"Coffee for you, sir," he said to Gideon as he thrust a coffee at him. "Three creams, no sugar, and pumpkin spice added." He looked quickly between the brothers before saying, "I took the liberty of canceling your next two appointments."

Gideon couldn't remember with whom he was supposed to meet, so he just nodded his head before taking a much-needed sip of coffee, the familiar rich aroma soothing.

"Pumpkin spice?" Gabriel quirked with distaste when the door closed.

"You got a problem with that?" Gideon responded in a no-nonsense tone.

Gabriel shook his head with a slightly amused look before looking down at Gideon's desk with a frown.

"You didn't answer the question," Gideon continued.

"What?" Gabriel looked up; his expression confused before it cleared. "No, I'm not sick."

"Is it Lily?" Gideon asked hesitantly, not sure how far to delve. "I saw her this morning with Nurse Summers and Eden."

"How did she seem?" his brother demanded, the intensity of his gaze surprising Gideon.

"Better—I mean happier," Gideon quickly amended his statement. "The three of them were hiding out from Mrs. Wright." He shrugged. "They seemed to be having fun."

Gabriel closed his eyes again. "This could not have happened at a worse time."

"What!" Gideon demanded, frustration seeping into his voice. The door behind him swung wide open, knocking into him, and causing him to spill hot coffee on his pants.

He cursed before he looked up to notice his father, who stared back at him with a scowl.

"Watch your language," his father commanded before closing the door and standing to the right of Gideon, who was ineffectually using a handkerchief to dab at his pants. Turning to Gabriel, the king asked, "Any word?"

Gabriel shook his head.

"What's going on?" Gideon brusquely interjected as he threw the handkerchief at his desk.

Both his brother and father looked away from him.

Gideon frowned as he considered that maybe the issue involved him. "Is it Angel?" he asked in a low tone.

"Are you going to play twenty questions all day," his brother asked, clearly irritated as he ran his hand over his head.

"I'll play one hundred questions until I get a response!" Gideon retorted.

"You can tell him," the king said to Gabriel.

"Funny," Gabriel said. "I was hoping you would." He turned to Gideon. "My son didn't die."

Gideon's head jerked back, and his whole body tensed. "But . . ." he began, only to stop at the sight of his brother's tears.

Their father moved around the desk and put his arm around his son's shoulders, saying emphatically, "We will find him." The king then looked at Gideon and finally explained, "Asier was born with a Tiger's claw on his face."

"Asier?" Gideon tilted his head. "Is that his name? But why does everyone say he's dead?"

The king sighed, dropping his arm from Gabriel who leaned his forehead into his hands.

"According to the Royal Rules of State," the king explained, "only my descendants 'without defects' can be in the line of succession."

"Then why is Gabriel next in line?" Gideon asked without thinking. At his father's and brother's incredulous looks, he mumbled, "Sorry about that. Back to Asier, your explanation didn't answer my question. Shouldn't he be here? Surely you don't believe the old superstition that those with a striped-shaped birthmark are inherently evil?"

Both his father and brother looked away from him.

"What did you do?" Gideon growled at his father, making a judgment call that his father was behind this situation. After all, he was trying to force him to marry Eden when she came of age, all to prevent islanders from figuring out the royal family secret: every one of them carried a gene that caused eyes to be completely white. Unnerving to look at, but relatively harmless if one protected the eyes from direct sunlight.

"Don't take that tone with me," his father replied, his tone as hard as Gideon's had been. "When you sit in my chair, you can tell me how to make choices. Are we clear?"

"Crystal," Gideon responded, consciously forcing his anger back.

"I should never have let him go," Gabriel said, slumping to sit in the chair, tears flowing down his face.

Seeing the misery on his brother's face, Gideon grabbed one of his guest chairs and pulled it right next to Gabriel. He sat down at an angle, and Gabriel turned in his seat so that they faced each other. Ignoring his father, whose right hand rested on Gabriel's right shoulder, Gideon leaned forward and said, "Tell me what happened."

His brother nodded. "It'll be a relief to tell someone." He leaned forward with his left hand resting on the desk. "Asier's birth was beautiful. I was there and cut the cord. He was the most wonderous sight I'd ever seen. Lily felt the same way. It was the three of us in our own little bubble." His brother paused, and his fist clenched on the desk.

"I wish I had met him," Gideon said softly.

"I really missed you that day," Gabriel said.

"I missed you too," Gideon replied, his voice choking a bit as he realized the truth of his words. He felt wetness on his own cheeks, which he hurriedly wiped away.

"So, when . . ." Gideon began, unsure how to continue.

"Mom came in," Gabriel said, his tone flat.

"Ugh," Gideon said in sympathy. "What did she say?"

"She told Lily that she had failed." Gabriel swallowed hard.

Gideon wiped his hand over his forehead as he slowly exhaled. *That explains Lily's mood swings*, he thought to himself. He loved his mother and thought he knew her, but this was a new low. He could only imagine what else she had said.

"What happened then?" Gideon encouraged when his brother paused. He braced himself to hear what else his mother had said. But his brother still didn't speak. He continued to sit with eyes closed, his body tense.

Gideon frowned and leaned closer, putting his hand on his brother's left shoulder. Their father still held on to Gabriel's right shoulder, and it was he who spoke next. "Asier was placed with a family in Untouchable City."

"To make it hard for Asier to be traced back to this house," Gideon spat back angrily as he looked up at his father. He regretted his impulsive outburst when Gabriel moaned.

"Sorry." He grimaced, giving his brother's shoulder what he intended to be a reassuring squeeze, but Gabriel winced.

"Stop squeezing, you two," he said.

"Oh," both the king and Gideon said as they quickly took their hands off Gabriel, who massaged first one shoulder and then the other, but his expression showed no relief.

"We have a contact with the family. They only know her as their part-time nanny. She got a message yesterday to take the next week off. We don't know where he is now." Gabriel's expression was bleak.

"It sounds like they plan to come back?" Gideon ventured.

"But what if they know who he really is?" Gabriel replied. "What do they intend to do with him? Or worse, what if they're being coerced into something because someone else knows who he is?"

Gideon jumped up. "You're right; we need to find him. What steps . . ."

"Sit down," his father interjected. "Everything that can be done is being done."

Gideon stayed standing, nearly biting his tongue in an effort not to say the whole thing was his father's fault. Only consideration for Gabriel stopped him from speaking.

The door to his office opened again and his mother entered, with Lily and Eden close behind. James followed them into the room, his expression grim. Gideon's heart sank as he took in Lily's wild-eyed expression.

"I overheard this royal guard state that the Raven had been located," she said as she stalked over to stand beside Gideon and look down at her husband with one hand on her hip. "Yes, I know that Raven is your code name for Asier. You couldn't even tell me he was missing?" Lily's face was a mask of anger and hurt.

Gabriel took a quick indrawn breath of relief as James gave a nod of confirmation. The king dismissed James, confusing Gideon as he wanted to know where his nephew had been located, but then his father walked to a corner of the room to make a call.

After James's exit, Gideon tilted his head toward the doorway where his assistant was doing a sort of shuffle with his feet and wringing his hands, not sure of the protocol. Fortunately, he picked up on Gideon's head tilt and hurriedly closed the door. Gideon made a mental note to remind him of his non-disclosure agreement.

Turning back to the situation at hand, he saw his father on his phone, presumably getting updates, while his mother stood with her arms crossed, her lips pinched, and her eyes cold.

Disturbed, Gideon looked at the source of her contempt, Lily, who was screaming at Gabriel, "I want to see my son now!" Turning to point at Eden who stood behind her, she continued, "If she can be here, why can't he?"

"Enough," Gideon's mother bit out, "before I slap you."

Eden gasped, while Lily stared at her mother-in-law, her eyes equally cold.

"Let's pray," the king said.

"I think . . . I think that's . . . a good idea," Eden stuttered out as she gripped her arms in a gesture that was becoming familiar to Gideon.

"I'm glad you think so," the king replied with a raised eyebrow, but there was humor in his voice.

Eden's face flushed red as she realized her blunder, but the king waived away her apologies.

The king insisted that they all hold hands as they stood. "Lord," he prayed, "we thank you for Asier's safe return and please guide us through the next steps."

"Amen," the others replied automatically.

The prayer was followed by a five-minute meditation that the king also insisted upon. Gideon wasn't sure how much meditation actually occurred. The queen and Lily exchanged chilly glances back and forth, and Gabriel looked with a pained gaze at his wife. Gideon felt an internal alarm go off as he looked at Eden, who stood stiffly, her upper arms squeezed tight to her sides as she bit at her chapped bottom lip. She seemed more worried than usual for her.

Finally, his father opened his eyes to an impatient audience. "Here's what we know: according to all reports, Asier's adoptive family dotes on him. All the neighbors report a seemingly happy family. They decided to take an impromptu trip to an amusement park with their nieces and nephews."

"Without letting anyone know?" Gabriel asked, his eyes narrowed.

"They don't know we're watching, remember?" his father replied.

Gabriel shook his head. "But things could have been wrong . . ."

"Tags have been added to everything possible so we can keep track of movements."

Gabriel nodded. "We should have thought to do that at the beginning."

"But can we see him—" Lily began, only to be cut off by her mother-in-law.

"Oh, not this again," the queen said.

"Actually, Jasmine, I'm leaning toward seeing him," the king replied with a frown, looking at his wife. "We rejected him out of pride and ego, and it's been eating at me ever since."

The queen looked at him wide-eyed. "But how?"

"A diplomatic visit," he replied.

"He's not on the island?" Lily exclaimed.

"He's in Untouchable City, in Saved America."

From there, the conversation moved into a detailed discussion about how to create a campaign with a "Year of the Child" theme that would explain a diplomatic visit to an organization well-known for assisting children and their families.

Gideon tuned out the conversation since Lily and Gabriel seemed fairly engaged. He planned to support them in whatever way they wanted. He was more worried about Eden, who was back to digging small incisions into her arms as she stared vacantly ahead.

"What's wrong?" he said quietly. They had long since all sat down in his conference room, the small table in his office not large enough to comfortably fit them all. Eden sat to his left.

In reply, Eden shook her head and looked down.

"We probably seem dysfunctional to you?" Gideon pushed.

Eden turned her head and locked gazes with him. "Your family is all here trying to solve a problem together."

Gideon finally put the pieces together. "I'm working on finding out what happened to your father and friends."

"Thanks," she said with a polite nod that left Gideon with no doubt that she didn't believe him.

Gideon clenched his jaw in frustration. He wanted to tell her exactly how much work he was doing for her, but so far his leads had petered out and he didn't want to give her false hope.

"Gideon and Eden, pay attention." His mother's strident voice cut through the noise in his head.

"What?" he mumbled.

"You're traveling with Gabriel and Lily to Untouchable City," his father replied.

5
EDEN, HEADING HOME

$\mathcal{F}$inally, I'd been released for my first royal family assignment. Gideon and I were traveling by plane with about fifteen other people, half of whom wanted to spend the ride giving me last-minute instructions. As I scrolled through my schedule, my whole being felt compressed into a space too small to contain me. I was going to explode. Or maybe disintegrate. I was like a ballerina made of ticker tape. The more I spun to please my new masters, the more pieces of me went flying off.

Suddenly antsy, I took off my button-down gray sweater and hugged myself. The voices on the plane were too loud and chatty. Feeling the dryness in the air and my throat, I took a sip of water. It sloshed uncomfortably in my stomach. I looked at the schedule again, dismayed at how little time I would have to myself in a country where I once had family and friends who loved me.

We were on our way to Untouchable City in Saved America. Two months after that awkward conversation with Gideon's family regarding Asier, it was finally arranged that the Royal Family Li would send representatives to the twentieth-anniversary celebration of the city's Resource and Research Center for Special Children and Adults. Four of us were the representatives: Gideon and I, as well as Gabriel and

Lily. Since the twins were not allowed to travel together, Gabriel and Lily traveled by separate plane.

"Are you ready, Ms. Edwards?" said an earnest voice.

I looked up to see the junior translator. She was talking to me, but she was frowning at Nurse Summers who sat next to me. I sighed, wondering why the islanders were so disturbed by the nurse's purple hair.

"Are you all right, nurse?" the translator asked.

Glancing sideways at Nurse Summers, I could see that the translator's concern had nothing to do with hair color. Nurse Summers's face was paler than normal. Her eyes were closed, but there was tension in the set of her mouth and in the stiff way she held her head. I tentatively touched her shoulder. "Do you need the doctor to come over?"

The nurse just shook her head and clutched her stomach. "Please don't touch me. Ate . . . something . . . bad."

"I can get the doctor," I said as I removed my arm.

"Already done," the translator said as the doctor came into view.

"I said no!" the nurse said sharply before slapping her hand over her mouth. She shoved the translator and doctor out of the way as she ran to the plane washroom.

The doctor followed the nurse, and the translator sat down in the seat vacated by the nurse.

The translator started talking, but my mind was on Nurse Summers. She had been distant the last couple of days, rarely looking directly at me. Maybe she was nervous about the trip too. Finally, I noticed the translator looking at me expectantly.

"I'm so sorry," I said. "I was thinking about the nurse. Can you please repeat what you said?"

"Blah, Blah, and Blah." That's not what she said, but that's what it sounded like to me.

"Translator," Gideon's voice interrupted.

I smiled in greeting, but she jumped up and gave him a bow.

"I need to go over some things with Eden," Gideon continued.

"Of course, sir," she said, moving quickly toward her seat a couple of rows back.

I shook my head as Gideon sat down next to me.

"What?" he asked.

"Everyone tries to please you," I replied, pushing my hair behind my ear.

"Have you met Gabriel?" he asked, his tone skeptical.

I laughed. "You know what I mean!"

"Here," he said, holding out one earbud. He put the matching one in his left ear.

"What is this?" I asked, taking the one he offered.

"It's an earbud," he replied with a blank expression.

"I know that!" I exclaimed, exasperated. "What am I listening to?"

"A lesson," he replied, his tone bored as he looked down at his electronic notepad.

"Great," I said, my bleak tone saying otherwise.

"You want me to go back over to my side of the plane?" he asked before giving me a mischievous grin. "I know you have a schedule and all."

I smiled back at him, the joy rising within me completely obliterating the despair of only moments ago. Our smiles deepened as we looked at each in understanding.

Confused by my urge to lean forward, I blinked and broke the connection. "So, you came over to rescue me from my schedule? A slow day for dragons?" I asked, fiddling with my own electronic notepad.

He laughed so loud that I jumped. Everyone looked at us with undisguised curiosity.

"Quiet down," I said, before I added for good measure, "Plus, I don't need rescuing."

"Look at your arms," he said quietly, his expression serious.

"Oh!" I inhaled sharply when I saw the indentations I had dug into my upper arms. I hurriedly put my sweater back on and placed the earbud in my right ear.

"OK, I'm ready for the lesson now," I said. I closed my eyes so I could focus.

Strange music filled my ear. The pace was very fast. As I continued to listen, it became clear that it was neither classical nor worship music.

With a gasp, I sat up and yanked out the earbud. With a surreptitious glance around, I whispered, "Am I supposed to listen to this?"

"Haven't you heard it before?" he asked, the surprise in his voice letting me know the music wasn't really a lesson.

"In my country, this sort of music isn't allowed," I replied, still holding the earbud with my fingers.

He stared at me for a long moment. "You are now a Seahorse Island citizen."

As I stared at him, he grimaced. "Okay, we won't listen to this music after we land, but did you hear what I said about being an island citizen?"

I nodded as a familiar worry bloomed. "And there's no way they can make me stay, right?"

"In Saved America?"

At my nod, he rolled his eyes. "No, you worry too much."

My skepticism must have shown on my face, as he had the good grace to look embarrassed. After all, he had been part of my security prep team and knew that I acquired enemies with unenviable ease. First, there was Mr. Brown, the morality inspector from my hometown of Sunny City, New Jersey. His own lack of morals forced my parents to send me away to school after years of homeschooling. The same school that I had to escape from after a couple of years due to the house I lived in being set on fire. Then, for reasons not made clear to me, a former employee of the Royal Family Li tried to have me kidnapped and sold before I could even get to the island. I still was irritated at the fact that Gideon would not share much information about the former employee, stating that they had to move carefully but that the betrayal would be handled. That's how he phrased it, as a betrayal of the royal family. His phrasing made me seem like a completely secondary concern.

As I remembered the conversation, something hard popped against my face. I had been mindlessly strangling the beaded bracelet on my wrist, and the thin plastic string had snapped. The pain on my wrist from the snap was sharp but quick. Still, I felt my face get hot with mortification as beads rolled on the floor of the plane. I moved to pick them up.

Gideon touched my shoulder. "Leave it; they have it."

I looked, and the plane staff were picking up the beads. I clenched my hands together and sat back in my seat.

Gideon placed his hands over my own. "Relax," he said. "You will never ever be alone on this trip. I would not have agreed to have you come along if I didn't think we could protect you."

If only he knew how many things I worried about. As the litany of worries began their familiar run-through in my mind, I removed my hands from Gideon's and my breath became shallow. Unable to be still, my fingers automatically moved to my bracelet before I remembered it was no longer there.

"Enough," Gideon said, pulling my gaze back to him. "When you meet your father again, do you want to tell him that you spent all this time crying? Or do you want to tell him what you accomplished?"

I wanted to say that my father didn't care about my accomplishments. He just loved me. But I didn't say anything. Gideon was correct that my father still wouldn't want me to spend all my time crying.

After a moment, I sighed. "I understand, but I have one last question. What about that woman in the video with the inspector? I'm worried that once I'm in Saved America, someone official will prevent me from leaving."

"We worked it out diplomatically," Gideon responded. "For right now, you are first and foremost a Seahorse Island citizen."

"The woman?"

"We have good intel that she's no longer an issue."

His casual confidence was both annoying and comforting. "That's good," I managed to get out.

"You ready to learn about the island's music?" Gideon asked, turning the conversation back to the start.

I rolled my eyes at him before I adjusted the earbud he'd given me earlier and leaned back. My eyes closed and my body relaxed as the music filtered through the chaos of my mind to focus my attention on its harmonious notes.

The first song had a slow melody. The singer's voice melded well with the music as he asked his love to stay with him till the very end. It was earnest and touching. I fell into a light sleep listening to it and began to dream.

I stood at the start of a long hallway with many doors. I knew the man for me was behind one of those doors, but which one? I tried one door and saw my father kneeling in front of my mother's grave. I moved to comfort him but was yanked back by some unseen force. The door slammed in my face. With tears in my eyes, I tried the door again, only to be yanked back even harder.

"Your only task is to find a husband. Keep looking!" a voice commanded.

The next door opened to Gabriel and Lily looking away from each other as they sat on a loveseat, the twins squalling unattended at their feet.

With a sigh, I went to the next door to see Queen Jasmine walking back and forth, apparently in the middle of a long speech. Her audience of one, the king, was asleep. I shook my head as I closed that door.

I looked around to see if there was something special about a door, a clue that would let me know which one to open. But all the doors were the same, so with another sigh, I went to the next one. Brother Adam and Ya Ya sat with hands clasped together, gazing adoringly at each other. I smiled at their obvious affection. Reluctantly, I closed the door.

"Which one is it, Eden?" the same voice as before mockingly asked. "You're running out of time. Tick-tock."

I opened door after door, but each remaining door opened to darkness. Finally, I was at the last door when I felt a touch on my arm. I jerked awake.

"We're almost there. We need to get ready," Gideon said brusquely, yanking the earbud out of my ear.

"What's wrong?" I said, holding my hand to my heart. It was still racing from the dream.

He leaned over to show me his phone. "Look," he said. A huge crowd of people stood behind a roped area. A lot of them had cameras.

"Journalists?" I asked.

He nodded. "Waiting at the airport for us. Apparently, they got wind of your presence."

I looked at him blankly.

He explained, "There's a lot of curiosity about a girl who was kidnapped from her parents and taken to Seahorse Island to eventually become a ward of the Royal Family Li. We can't completely avoid the press, but we will do what we can to avoid them."

"They think my father is dead?" I asked.

He nodded.

I pushed down the panic at the thought of my father being dead. The made-up narrative was too close to my fears. I closed my eyes against the unthinkable.

"Just breathe," Gideon whispered in my ear.

As I slowly exhaled, I remembered my lessons on dealing with the press. "But all I have to do is walk past them, smile, and wave?"

"Who? Oh, the press? That's exactly right," he said as he smiled, holding up a pair of shades. "And wear these."

"It's winter. Why would I wear shades in the winter?" I asked.

"Shades make me look even cooler," he said, still holding the shades out to me.

I looked closely to see if he was joking, but he wasn't.

I took the glasses. "I guess it can help with the glare. Let me find Nurse Summers." I stood up to move.

"Wait," Gideon said. "She's still sick. I will escort you. Besides, the team needs to get you ready." He gestured behind me.

The next thirty minutes were awkward. I had to stop the stylist from coming into the washroom with me. She relented once I reassured her that I could get dressed by myself. Her taste was admirable, though. She had chosen a deep burgundy sweater to go with a microsuede skirt of the same color.

After I got dressed, however, my right to privacy ended. One person redid my hair back into a bun, while at the same time, someone else redid my makeup. The stylist readjusted my clothing. My assigned liaison reviewed out loud the structure of Saved America's government. I refrained from yelling that I had been raised there.

"Ten minutes!" someone yelled, and everyone moved away except the stylist. She provided me with a long wool espresso-colored coat and matching boots.

"Where's her purse?" she yelled as I put on the boots.

"In my seat," I said, panting from wrangling my feet into the boots.

"Here!" Someone shoved a burgundy clutch purse at me that I had never seen before.

"But . . ." I pointed to my old purse.

"Look in the purse in your hand," the stylist said a bit impatiently. Of course, all my stuff had been moved from my old purse to this new more stylish one.

I frowned at the lack of privacy, but it was time to sit back in our seats for the plane to actually land.

Once we deplaned, the sheer noise and excitement from the waiting crowd immobilized me. I stood at the top of the stairs, all dressed up with my cool shades, going absolutely nowhere. I could see my breath as my face stung from the cold.

"You've got your shades; you're cool," Gideon whispered. "Hold on to me."

Taking another deep breath, I did as he bid, and we walked down the steps together. As we walked past the crowd, Gideon smiled and waved, and I did the same. I heard my name screamed and tried not to react. Gideon kept walking, but he put his hand over the hand I was using to hold on to his arm. I looked at him with a grateful smile before I turned back and continued waving to the crowd.

"ARE YOU OKAY?" Nurse Summers asked me a few days later as we toured the resource center we had come to see. In our core group were Gideon, Nurse Summers and me, a few translators, and a diplomatic liaison. Lily and Gabriel should have been with us, but they had met Asier and his adoptive parents the day before—as the island's emissaries, not his birth parents—and Lily had been crying ever since. But even without Lily and Gabriel, the group was large. Our tour guide, the director of the school, was accompanied by the entire board of trustees, making it more likely that even whispered statements could be overheard. So, I just gave the nurse a tight smile in return and remained silent.

In actuality, I was disturbed. I'd lived for years with the unacknowledged belief that the virus was the sole cause of children born with differences. Thus, if one could avoid the virus by avoiding mosquitoes or using a surrogate, the end result would be a perfect baby. I never once wondered what would happen if the baby was, well, imperfect. Now I knew that a lot of those babies ended up here, in this school created for them.

After I got past the shock of seeing children who walked, talked, or moved differently, it became apparent that they were fiercely loved. In preparation for our visit, some of the older children prepared essays, and I noticed some of their mothers tear up as they read about how the school had made their lives better. They all had jobs lined up for when they graduated. As I clapped for the last student who read, I felt something expand within me, something I hadn't even had the sense to realize was too small.

As the school director came on stage to rejoin the older students, I felt a tapping on my thigh. A dark-haired little boy with the most mischievous grin was holding onto my thigh as he stood in the aisle. With his other hand, he held out crushed orange slices to me, juice from the fruit sliding down his hand onto the floor.

"Aw!" I said, accepting his sticky gift, only to have him grasp my face in his two now-empty hands and laugh happily.

His joy was infectious, and I wanted to laugh too, but the director was still speaking, so I put my finger to my still-smiling lips.

"My apologies," a harried-looking woman said as she picked him up.

"He's lovely," I whispered to her, surreptitiously wiping my face just as the auditorium lights flicked back on and guests began to disburse.

"He's too excited," she said with exasperation. "He doesn't understand that he can't join his sister on stage."

"What's your name?" I asked the little boy as I stood and moved to the aisle.

He just giggled and turned to bury his face in his mother's neck. She shook her head, gave me a small wave, and went to find her daughter.

I turned to Gideon to see if he had seen the cute little boy, but his face was completely unreadable.

"Are you okay?" I asked him.

"I know he's not Asier, a little too young, but this whole charade is bothering me. Let's shake hands and get back to the hotel," he replied, not looking at me.

I hurriedly dumped the orange slices into the nearest trash receptacle, wincing as I did so. I should have told the little boy that I could not accept his gift.

I fumbled through the first few introductions. It didn't help that I felt unequal to the mothers I met. I had spent weeks practicing how to do meet-and-greets smoothly, whereas these women went on raising children who society, to a large extent, despised. Equally disturbing, I saw no fathers. I tried to remind myself that they could be at work. But I wondered if they had rejected their children because they knew that many would.

I felt very small and mean, because I couldn't lie to myself that I would have been any different if not for my visit to this school. It was just like when I'd closed my eyes against the suffering of the companions at my old high school. I had been grateful that I wouldn't suffer the degradation they would. Never once had I thought to help them. I couldn't remember if I'd even prayed for them. I felt my face flush as we all headed toward the door where the security team was waiting.

"You seem lost in your thoughts?" Gideon inquired with a raised eyebrow, bringing me out of my reverie.

I was walking between him and Nurse Summers. I looked at him, but he was frowning, looking past me to her.

"I didn't say anything," she whispered to him.

Before I could say anything, one of the royal guards yelled, "Code M!"

That code meant to move ahead of the media due to the danger of a media swarm, where a bunch of media types surround the target asking question after question, hoping to get good footage of their target looking bad or disoriented. Royal charm was generally ineffective in dispelling them. They didn't want to be charmed. They wanted destruction suitable to feed humankind's insatiable appetite for schadenfreude and packaged for the shortest attention span. The worst part was the security risk that someone with ill intent could be in the media crowd, which depending on the size could make it more difficult for security to rescue you. I had never experienced a Code M, only trained for it. The school was only supposed to have limited media presence.

"Excuse me, how does it feel to be returned home?" an unfamiliar voice said next to me.

Confused, I turned to them, barely missing the outstretched microphone in their hand, only to have someone else touch my arm on the other side.

"Were you really kidnapped?" the other person asked. This person too was fond of jabbing microphones in others' faces.

When I felt a third person touch my back, I understood why Code M was called. Understanding didn't help the panic though. I turned to Gideon who grabbed my hand and started running, pulling me with him. Once outside, I blinked against the glare of the sun reflecting off the vehicle in front of us.

"Get in!" Gideon shouted, practically throwing me into the back seat and following close behind.

A hand pounded on the window. I turned to see a raised camera, but then the car jerked, and we were moving.

"What happened?" I asked, turning to look out the back window. My racing heart sped up even more at the sight of so many cameras pointed at our car. I quickly turned back around.

"They can't see us through the glass," Gideon said, leaning forward and slightly sideways to see out the front window. His hand tightened around mine.

"Luke," he said to the driver, "what's the situation at the hotel?"

"More vultures," Luke replied as he maneuvered the vehicle behind the others along a stretch of road made narrow by throngs of people.

Gideon swore. "The barriers should have been set further back."

"You don't say," Luke responded sarcastically.

"We're sitting ducks," I said, not quite keeping the tremble from my voice.

Gideon turned to me. "In about fifteen minutes, there will be a blind spot. You and I are going to get out and run up a flight of stairs."

"The hell you will," Luke exclaimed, making a sharp turn.

"Sir—" the other royal guard in the car began.

"Luke and Matthew, the plan wasn't a suggestion," Gideon said, using a hard tone I'd never heard him use.

"Eden?" He turned to me.

I nodded reluctantly, trusting that he wasn't leading us straight into more media.

"Good girl," he said and literally patted me on the head.

I gaped at him, but he had turned away to yell instructions to the driver. But, seriously, was I a dog?

Turning my attention to my surroundings, I watched mute as the line of cars carrying us, Nurse Summers, security, and staff moved fluidly through traffic. It was more like twenty minutes when we came to a stop and Gideon pulled me out of the car, telling me to keep my head down low.

We entered the back door of a building and ran up about twenty flights of stairs. I thought he said one flight. I was completely out of breath by the time we finally exited the stairwell. My heart lifted as I saw the bridge that led directly to our hotel.

"Only a little bit more," Gideon urged.

As we ran the length of the bridge, some of the security team became visible in front of the doors at the end of the bridge.

We were almost there when a drone appeared in front of us.

6

GIDEON, LETTING GO

The drone paused in midair, whirring as a telescopic lens protruded in the direction of Gideon and Eden. They both stopped abruptly and looked desperately behind them for an escape route, only to see another media horde storming toward them.

"This way!" a voice yelled, and they looked back toward the hotel bridge's double doors.

They ran toward the doors, and as soon as they stepped inside, security slammed and locked the doors against the media, which immediately banged on them. Security hustled Gideon and Eden back to the royal hotel suite. After security had checked and double-checked the premises, Gideon asked them to leave.

As soon as security left, Gideon and Eden sat together on the suite's uncomfortable sofa, still stunned by the day's events. Before they could muster up the energy to talk through anything, Gabriel and Lily arrived with the royal guards, Luke and James.

"That was a complete cluster," Luke stated as he strode in. He pointed to Eden but looked to Gideon. "We didn't have the information we needed to do our jobs!"

"That's an excuse!" Gideon yelled back as he stood. "You weren't protecting her at all!"

Gabriel held up a hand to stop them from the back and forth. Looking at his watch phone, he said, "The Comms Minister is saying that searches on Eden's name are way up. Lots of searches on whether she is an American citizen and whether she should be with an American family." He looked back up.

"This is orchestrated," Lily said. She had squeezed in between Gideon and Eden on the sofa and had one arm around Eden, who still looked a bit shocked. "Bringing her along was media gold; everyone loves a Cinderella story. She's an orphan who comes from a humble background to become a ward of the royal family. She makes us look good." Lily seemed surprised when Eden shook off her arm and left the room.

"Honey," Gabriel began, "where are you going with this?"

"I mean that's the story the media should be running with, and the fact that they are not is because someone else wants them to tell a different story."

"Exactly," Gabriel said. "Generate enough interest, then the government is forced to intervene. They place her with a family in Saved America. But for what reason?"

"Money," Luke replied. "After all, you bought her. Somebody else might . . ."

"Stop talking, Luke," Gabriel commanded, wishing he had been quicker as he noticed his brother's face contorted in a mask of frustration.

"We are leaving," Gideon said. "I'm taking her back to the island. Lily and Gabriel can stay to finish the visit."

A WEEK LATER, Gideon paused the video footage he had been viewing. It was weird to see the larger-than-life, black-and-white freeze-frame image of Eden and him running on the bridge. Eden's hair had become undone, curls streaming behind her, glinting under the cold sun of winter. Her breath in the wintry air was visible on the screen, the resolution so clear that he almost shivered from a phantom chill. This footage must have been the last image captured before the staffer who had yelled at them to run through the doors had grabbed the drone and crushed it between his massive hands.

Gideon returned his attention to his father and Gabriel. The three of them were in his father's conference room. Gabriel's eyes were reddened from lack of sleep, and his hair was tousled every which way. Gideon knew he didn't look much better. He loosened his tie even further as he glanced at his father sitting at the head of the table, the circles under his eyes even deeper than they had been during the Angel situation.

The week since their return to the island had been good media-wise, but the drone created unease. Until now, they didn't know who sent it and for what purpose. They were watching *The Glitter Tattle's* teaser on a one-hour special on Gideon and Eden's "forbidden relationship." Gideon winced at the astounding number of views just for the teaser alone.

"I don't believe this," Gabriel muttered as Jack and Gwen, the show's hosts, appeared on the screen.

"We've done all we can do to mitigate this story," his father said wearily, running a hand across his face. "A few tailored stories here and there should not worry us."

"But *The Glitter Tattle* has a viewership in the millions," Gabriel exclaimed.

"Then Communications will handle it," their father snapped back.

"Of course," Gabriel replied, but he shot a worried glance across the table to Gideon.

Gideon understood his brother's concern. While their Minister of Communications was a veritable magician at getting unpleasant stories to disappear, she could only do so much. The island media had run stories on the positive facets of their diplomatic trip to the Untouchable City in Saved America. The images were touching, often showing the momentary and unscripted connections between the royals and the children they were visiting. On the web, though, their numbers showed that plenty of island citizens were actively consuming stories from the UK media which focused on Gideon and Eden, and the spin was more salacious than positive, relying more on pure conjecture than facts. Today, though, was the first day they had seen footage from the incident on the bridge.

"I'm tired." Gabriel stood abruptly. "Fill me in later," he said as he strode from the conference room, slapping Gideon on the back as he went out.

"I don't want to be here either," Gideon muttered to himself, earning a pointed glare from his father.

Gideon splayed his hands and raised his shoulders in the universal symbol of confusion. "I just thought the crown prince would want to be involved in all serious matters involving the family."

His father leaned forward. "And I would have thought he could have relied on his twin brother these past two years."

Gideon's jaw tightened at his father's verbal jab.

After a tense silence, his father said, "This day has been too long. We'll watch this trivia in the morning."

Gideon was still miffed from before, but he nodded, thinking it wiser to keep silent.

As he and his father made their way upstairs to their respective suites, Gideon mentally arranged the next day's schedule. He needed to check in with his field team regarding Eden's father. They had found him and extracted him and had a plan for how to move forward. He needed to decide whether to prep Eden.

Something of his distress must have shown on his face. His father reached out and clasped Gideon's shoulder. "We'll get through this," he said.

"I know," Gideon replied.

His father smiled slightly, easing the severity of his face. As they got closer to their suites, the unmistakable sound of laughter echoed through the hall.

"Is everyone still up?" Gideon asked.

Their individual suites were located behind a large family room situated directly in front of the atrium on the top floor of the palace. The family room walls were done in soft blue and white, the predominant colors of the island's flag. When father and son reached the room, they saw that everyone was indeed still up.

Eden and Ya Ya sat on the floor in front of the green plants stretching to reach the sunlight that would come through the atrium glass during the day. They were playing some sort of card game. Queen Jasmine was sitting in a gold and light blue striped chair to their left, reading a book. She preferred an actual book to a screen for bedtime reading. A small end table separated the queen from Brother Adam who sat in a matching chair with his eyes closed and his legs elevated on a small ottoman in front of him.

Across from the queen and Brother Adam, Lily and Gabriel sat close together on an overlarge sofa. Gabriel's arm was around Lily's shoulders, while his other arm held a sleeping Amara. Lily was holding Aditya. The baby was not yet sleeping, but her eyes were slowly opening and closing, and she chewed voraciously on the pacifier in her mouth, drool dripping down her chin. Her eyes widened when she saw her uncle.

Gideon opened his mouth to speak, but his brother shook his head. The whole room stayed silent until Aditya's eyes finally remained closed. They all looked sheepishly at each other while Gideon and his father sat on a loveseat near the door.

"I can't believe we're letting that baby dictate how the palace is run," Queen Jasmine said archly with a look at Lily.

To Gideon's surprise, Lily gave a rueful smile and said, "She takes after her grandmother."

The queen laughed and looked at her daughter-in-law with something close to respect. "I never thought of it that way. Come on, Eden. We'll put the twins to bed so Gabriel and Lily can have a little time together."

"Oh no," Lily started to protest, but Gabriel shushed her and whispered something in her ear. Lily blushed and changed her stance. "Thank you, Mother," she said and bowed her head slightly.

Gideon wondered at the change in Lily since their trip. He had wanted to bring Asier back to the palace, but Lily had shaken her head reluctantly at the idea. "He is happy and loved here," she had said. "To take him away from his family would cause him trauma."

Gideon had vehemently disagreed. He had given examples of families reunited with their kidnapped children. In hindsight, his examples were not chosen wisely.

His sister-in-law had replied, "In all those cases, a child was forcibly taken or somehow taken without the agreement of the parents. You've provided no examples in which the family basically gives the kid away and then changes their mind."

He shook off the unhappy memory and turned his attention back to his family, watching as Eden stood up, a mulish expression on her face.

"Yes, Eden, go help with the twins," Ya Ya concurred with her daughter-in-law. "You don't know how to play this game."

By the look on Eden's face, Gideon guessed that Ya Ya was cheating.

"Are you cheating, Ya Ya?" he called out.

"Come help me up so I can beat you," she replied, raising one fist into the air.

Gideon threw back his head and laughed, some of the tenseness from the past weeks loosening.

THE NEXT MORNING Gideon got up an hour earlier than usual and dragged his tired body down to the lower level for a swim. Blearily, he opened the pool door, only to find Eden sitting on a deck bench. She was sitting up but asleep, her head slumped down, still in her flamingo-patterned pajamas. He vaguely remembered her getting them on a shopping trip with Lily during their time in Saved America.

He let the door close, and her head jerked up. "You're here," she said before stretching her arms upward and yawning without covering her mouth.

"Cover your mouth," he commanded with an exaggerated shake of his head. "Don't they teach you anything?"

She rolled her eyes. "I miss Nurse Summers." She slouched down before continuing. "I'm stuck with Mrs. Wright."

Gideon swore inwardly. He couldn't tell her the truth about Nurse Summers. "She had to return to the UK for work."

Eden's mouth twisted. "I'm not sure that is the case," she said hesitantly. "That's actually why I'm down here."

Gideon's hand hesitated on the towel he was reaching for. "What's going on?"

"I think she knew whoever wanted the media to chase us," she said haltingly. "Or at least I think I do. But I don't think Nurse Summers was in on it."

Gideon's skepticism must have shown on his face.

"No, really, she had been acting so weird that when she slipped away from the group, I followed her and—"

"After all that training . . ." Gideon was so mad he could not speak. This was new information to him. He was angry at himself for not noticing her absence at the time. He'd had many conversations during the tour at the school, and he could not say he'd always kept track of Eden's whereabouts. He trusted their security team, but they should have advised her against slipping away. She had placed herself in danger. Nurse Summers could easily have turned that small mistake into a bigger problem.

Eden cringed. "I know it was a breach of protocol, especially since we were representing the island."

Gideon shook his head as he sat next to her. "I'm talking about security training. If she was working with someone else, you could have been seriously harmed."

Eden's face twisted a moment. "You're right. I wasn't thinking."

"Clearly!" Gideon agreed.

At her stricken expression, he softened his voice. "What happened when you followed her?"

"She was on her phone with someone. I didn't mean to overhear, but her voice was so . . ." Eden paused.

"Go on," Gideon encouraged, tamping down his impatience.

"She was desperate. I knew from before that her mother was dead.

After listening for a minute, I think she was on the phone with her father. I went to move away; it seemed voyeuristic to continue listening."

"But . . ." Gideon prompted, leaning forward.

"She said to the person on the phone that they kept asking her about me, but she didn't come to the island for some stupid babysitting gig." Eden made a rueful face.

"She said that?" Gideon asked as he watched the light reflections from the pool ripple across her face. He could not gauge her mood.

"Yes, she did." Eden looked at him. "I heard her say that the person on the phone used to work for your father. She called him Chief Sims kind of sarcastically, but it seemed like he hung up on her."

"What happened then?" Gideon asked, leaning forward. His father's investigators had uncovered the hidden familial tie with the former Chief, but they could not confirm if the nurse had been working with him on some sort of scheme.

"Nothing, I just slipped back into the group. What about Chief Sims?"

"He no longer works for the family," Gideon replied. "You think she was sending information to him."

Eden nodded. "It didn't register at first, her words. But she acted so different from that point—like she would never look me in the face—that I started rethinking everything that happened. I may be misreading the situation."

Gideon held up his hand. "No, don't second-guess yourself. You did the right thing in telling me. To be honest, we had found out a bit about her background. Remember when we were in Saved America and she told me she didn't say anything?"

Eden tilted her head as she tried to retrieve the memory. "I remember now. I wondered at that time what she was referring to, but then I forgot to ask you about it."

"Gabriel and I had asked some questions about her connection to former Chief Sims," he admitted. "I asked her to keep it quiet. How do you feel about her leaving the island?"

"Falls under the category of things I don't like but I understand."

At Gideon's raised eyebrow, Eden explained, "If I had to betray someone to live with my dad again, I can't say I would not do it. Was this former Chief involved in what happened in England?"

Gideon debated internally how much to tell her.

"If you can't tell me now, can you tell me later?" she asked.

Relieved, Gideon nodded. They both jumped when the door opened.

"Prince Gideon," his assistant, Tim Plath, called to him. "Your morning appointment is here."

Exasperated, Gideon snapped at his assistant, "I don't have a morning appointment."

"You told me to add your new liaison to the schedule as soon as it was possible," his assistant replied.

Gideon had been planning to check on the status of his new liaison that morning, not meet with the person. He was going to have to miss his swim completely. "I'll be there in thirty minutes. Give him my apologies for being late."

Plath's eyes widened in alarm, and he tilted his head meaningfully.

"He's behind you?" Gideon said as he stood.

Plath nodded, the relief evident on his face. "I assumed you wanted to see him as soon as he arrived."

The man in question stepped around Plath and bowed to Gideon. "Steve Mann, reporting for duty, Your Highness," he said in English. Gideon noticed the slight limp and winced.

"You're American!" Eden gasped, jumping up and coming to stand in front of Mr. Mann. "Which parts?"

"Eden," Gideon chastised gently. He introduced Eden as the royal family's ward, expecting her to give a brief bow back to his guest.

Instead, Eden tilted her head to the side and asked, "Have we met before?"

Gideon felt sweat rivulets run down the side of his face, doubting if he could blame part of it on the pool room being overly heated. Would she recognize Mr. Mann as her father right away? Extensive cosmetic surgery had changed her father's face, but coming up with a cover story for his American accent took some work.

"No, Ms. Edwards. I was raised in England, but my mother was American."

"Which explains the accent," Eden said with a smile.

"Mr. Mann is here as our new diplomatic liaison for Saved America and South America," Gideon explained.

Eden nodded and, after an awkward silence, excused herself. "I should go and get ready for the day."

An hour later, Gideon was having coffee with Mr. Mann. They were sitting at a small two-person table on the main level right next to the ceiling-to-floor window, making inconsequential small talk.

"Thank you for everything," Mr. Mann interjected at one point.

Gideon nodded, saying nothing else. Palace staff were trained to be discreet, but he did not want to tempt fate. A special team had extracted Eden's father from his tormentors. The extraction team wore cameras that captured the swing of a wooden bat repeatedly hitting one of her father's legs before the interrogators were killed. Gideon's face hardened as he remembered Mr. Mann screaming, "I don't know!"

The irony of the situation was that Mr. Mann's tormentors were asking how to get to Eden in the palace. He did not, in fact, know the answer to the question, but he had been rescued and brought to the palace.

"The decision was made to take her on the Saved America trip?" Mr. Mann inquired, looking directly at him.

Gideon paused in picking up his coffee. While Mr. Mann reported to him, he was also Eden's father. "We didn't know the media would be so interested."

Mr. Mann looked away. "The trouble in Saved America is that perhaps there was more than one buyer interested in the transaction."

Gideon slammed his coffee down, ignoring the burning sensation as some of it sloshed over the rim onto his hand. "I underestimated the efforts others would exert to have a girl with Eden's profile. That will not happen again."

"Good," her father replied, looking him directly in the eye.

"I'm sorry you had to experience . . ." Gideon motioned with his hand to the other man's legs. "I wish we could have gotten you out sooner."

"It is what it is," Mr. Mann replied before taking a sip of his coffee. "What about the media?"

"They are always a problem. We'll just have to make sure the Americans, the media, and whoever else understand that she is with family now."

"Is she?" Mr. Mann queried, an unspoken challenge in his eyes.

"Yes," Gideon responded, not lowering his own eyes.

"You intend to marry her?" the other man asked.

Gideon spit out the small sip of coffee he had just taken. "No, she's like a sister to me."

Mr. Mann wiped off the drops of coffee that had splattered his immaculate suit. "Why the news stories about her?"

Gideon shrugged. "Most of the articles are about whether she should be returned to Saved America. Not surprisingly, none of their so-called facts come close to reality."

Noticing the look of quiet fury on the other man's face, Gideon leaned forward. "Don't worry. The Minister of Communications is getting the story we want out there."

"Your Communications person is going to stop them from calling her an—uhm—unmentionable word?"

"No one is calling her a . . . No one's calling her that," Gideon said, all cordiality gone from his voice. He wondered if he'd made a mistake bringing Eden's father onboard.

Noting the consternation on the prince's face, Mr. Mann pulled out a screen and gave it a verbal command. Once the theme music for *The Glitter Tattle* came on, he positioned the screen so that both of them could see it as it revealed the two hosts, Rianne and Tyler, looking like younger versions of the main hosts, except with reddish and black hair instead of the ubiquitous blond and much less Botox.

"We're sitting in for Jack and Gwen," Rianne began as the camera zoomed in on the hosts sitting at the long newscasters' desk.

"They'll be back tonight," Tyler cut in as Rianne's conspiratorial smile froze. "But we wanted our viewers to have the most up-to-date information on the Edengate situation."

"Tyler," Rianne cut in with a bright smile. "Let us introduce our guest today, Mr. Schill, an expert on American culture." The camera focused on a dapper silver-haired gentleman dressed in a tweed jacket over a cashmere sweater. He sat closest to Rianne. The bottom of the screen read, *Dr. Phil Schill, professor of North American culture at the University of Melbourne.*

"Mr. Schill," Tyler began. "What do you make of Eden Edwards's story that she was kidnapped?"

The man in question nodded sagely. "Women in Saved America, especially unmarried girls, are kept under tight control."

"So, it would be impossible for her to have been kidnapped?" Rianne asked, leaning toward the show's guest and turning her back slightly to Tyler.

"Not impossible, but improbable." Mr. Schill looked back and forth from the camera to Rianne. "Unless. . ." Here he paused.

Now both Rianne and Tyler were leaning toward him. "Please continue," they both said.

"I hate to spread any rumors," Mr. Schill demurred. "But Saved America does, unfortunately, have a history of training unmarried young women as companions."

"That's a sex worker?" Tyler asked.

"Oh, my!" Rianne sat up even straighter as she looked at the camera with her eyes wide as if in shock.

"Is that possible in this case?" Tyler pressed. "Is . . ." He paused to look at his notes.

"Eden," Rianne hissed out with a smile. "Hence, Edengate?"

"Thanks, Rianne," Tyler continued unperturbed. "Professor, what are your thoughts?"

"I think her story sounds a bit implausible, but I admire her for coming up with a new way to meet a prince!" He shared a laugh with the entertainment hosts before shaking his head. "It's almost unfathomable that she would have been kidnapped."

Across the screen the phrase *Fraudulent Orphan?* appeared below the black-and-white image of Gideon and Eden running across the hotel bridge in Saved America.

"Vultures, all of them," Gideon muttered to himself as he paced the confines of his suite, his mind reluctantly replaying *The Glitter Tattle* show from earlier. He desperately needed sleep, but he knew he would not be able to rest. Even though it was almost midnight, his anger was still riding him. He had spent the day on damage control, and now his brain could not shut off. In the military, he had learned to distance himself from his emotions, but no amount of meditation or deep breathing exercises would help him now.

He hurriedly undressed out of his suit, feeling freer as he redressed into a pair of old shorts and a T-shirt, and headed down to the unused pool room. Thirty minutes into a solitary game of pool, Gideon could finally feel himself calming.

He leaned over to push the eight ball into the corner pocket. Satisfied with his performance, he methodically retrieved the balls and centered them on the table. He could not remember the last time he had been in this room. Originally intended as extra storage space, he and Gabriel had claimed it as a hangout spot when they turned thirteen.

"What is wrong with your lovely playroom?" their mother had asked, one hand clutching a strand of pearls while the other hand rested on her hip. She was standing at the entrance to the room.

"We're too old for a playroom!" Unfortunately, Gideon's voice had cracked on the declaration.

His heart had sunk at the set look on her face. He could just tell she was going to nix their hangout spot, but then his father had joined her.

"Nice work," he had said, looking around approvingly.

Their mother started to protest, but their father claimed he needed her advice on something, and she immediately shifted her focus to him.

Gideon smiled as he remembered that interaction. He and Gabriel had felt so grown-up since they had succeeded in claiming the room as theirs. Now he noticed the stale smell, dingy off-white walls, and plain furnishings. In addition to the pool table in the center of the admittedly small room, a couple of hard plastic chairs lined one wall with a mini refrigerator between them that also served as a table.

He sat in one of the chairs and opened the refrigerator, finding it stocked with bottles of club soda and one bottle of liquor. One of the many bottles he had pilfered from formal palace events in his teen years. The thrill of sneaking it past the adults and the Royal Snitches had been intoxicating. Desire, strong and sure, surged through him, and his hand reached out of its own volition.

"You are a drunk and a klepto!" He heard the words in his ear as if his brother were shouting them now and not years ago in the past.

He hurriedly grabbed a soda and slammed the door shut. Frowning, he sipped the soda until his hands were steady again. He had sworn off alcohol when he was banished from the island. He had encountered alcohol since then, but he had not been as tempted as he was just moments before. His cheeks burned as he remembered his brother's disgust in their teen years. Gideon had thrown up all over Gabriel more than once as his brother had tried to sneak him back to their rooms.

"Lord, help me," he whispered, eyes closed, as memories of his past taunted him.

"This is where you are?" a familiar voice said.

Gideon opened his eyes to see his brother standing in the doorway. At Gideon's nod of acknowledgment, Gabriel sat in the other chair, leaning forward, his hands touching at the fingertips.

The brothers sat in silence until Gideon realized he was falling asleep. He shook himself to wake up and then reached over, using the back of his hand to lightly tap his brother's arm. "Thanks for checking in on me."

Gideon stood up, stretched his arms wide, and yawned. He started to walk toward the door but realized Gabriel was still sitting and frowning.

Gideon winced as he rubbed his back. "Let's catch up at breakfast tomorrow?"

Gabriel nodded slowly and stood up as well. But then he said, "You fought hard for Eden today."

Gideon shook his head. "I'm not understanding. Let's talk and walk."

As the brothers reached the door together, Gideon looked slyly at his brother, whose turn it was to shake his head.

"We are grown men. We are not doing this!"

When they were younger, they would fight over who entered or exited first through the narrow doorway.

Today, though Gabriel claimed to be grown, he took a flying leap toward the door, only to be blocked by his brother's elbow. He responded by tripping Gideon, who pulled Gabriel down with him.

"What is this!" cried a shrill voice. Their mother stood in front of them. She looked from one to the other accusingly.

Both brothers jumped to their feet, ready to apologize, but their mother's hand went up in the universal stop gesture.

"Act like I raised you!" she commanded before regally stalking away.

"You started this!" Gabriel hissed at Gideon; his voice low to avoid reaching their mother.

"Really?" Gideon asked, incredulously. "I was down here all by my lonesome, and then someone came to join me!"

"You're the one acting like you're going to marry that girl!"

Stupefied, Gideon picked up his club soda and made a big show of turning the bottle slowly. "Did you add alcohol to this? Because I can't make sense of what you just said."

"Look, the plan changed from schooling her within the palace to sending her away to school to avoid some of the negative press, but then you came in and insisted—until we got sick of arguing with you—that we stick with the original plan. Why would you do that?"

"When I marry, it will be to someone who is actually an adult and not a kid. Eden is a kid who desperately needs her new family to stand by her," Gideon declared and walked away from the door. He turned for one final parting shot. "How many negative articles came out about Lily? You want to send her away too?"

Immediately, Gideon could tell he had gone too far.

Gabriel glared at him, nostrils flaring, fists clenched. "Lily is my wife, you imbecile!"

"And Eden is family!" Gideon yelled back as he walked away.

"She's temporary family, not real family," Gabriel said as he followed Gideon around a corner and stopped abruptly. Eden stood there.

"Gide, I . . ." Gabriel began.

"Shut up!" Gideon retorted, his heart sinking as he took in Eden's pale face and stooped shoulders.

Gabriel pressed his lips together and walked away.

"He's a jack—" Gideon's swearing was cut off by Eden pressing her palm firmly against his mouth, her eyes wide.

"Cursing is not allowed in the palace!" she exclaimed.

Removing Eden's hand from his mouth and holding it, Gideon asked, "Who told you that lie?"

"Mrs. Wright," Eden replied and then reddened. "There's no such rule, is there?"

"Technically, no," Gideon replied with an amused smile. "It's just not expected."

"Still, he's family," she said and looked down.

"And you are too," Gideon replied forcefully, tightening his hand on hers.

Eden kept looking at the floor. "Is Mr. Mann who I think it is?"

Gideon sucked in a breath. "You know?"

She raised her tear-stricken face and nodded. "I—"

"No, don't tell me," Gideon said as he pulled her in for a hug and whispered, "His life depends on everything being secret."

She nodded, but he could feel fresh tears falling onto his shirt.

"Can you act as though you don't know?" he asked.

"Yes," she replied, her voice wavering.

He moved to let her go, but she held on. "Thank you so much. I'm sorry for doubting you."

"I'm still not done on . . . the others," he replied, meaning Kaitlyn and Bethany.

"I trust you," she said, stepping out of the hug and giving him a tiny smile.

He started to smile back, but he heard a nearby floorboard creak.

"I think it's Mrs. Wright," Eden said in a panicked whisper.

He put his finger to his lips and then quickly pulled them both into a nearby supply closet, gently locking the door. They slipped down to avoid the small window at the top. The silence seemed to almost pulse with expectation as they gazed at each other's shadowed faces using the limited light from the hallway. They dared not take any audible breaths.

Gideon put his finger to his mouth again.

I got it! Eden mouthed.

Gideon made a zipping motion with his hand across his mouth and then pointed to his watch phone. He pulled out his regular phone and muted it as well. He pointed at her, but she shook her head.

Finally, they heard the steps move away. Eden moved to get up, but Gideon pulled her back down just as the hallway went dark. After an interminable period, they slowly exited, laughing sheepishly as the lights came back on.

"Motion sensors," Eden muttered.

Gideon chuckled too, but he felt uneasy.

LATER THAT NIGHT, he dreamed of the knitting girl again. At the beginning of the dream, she sat with her head down, the sun streaming in through window blinds creating a glow behind her and highlighting her curls. The red scarf grew longer and longer as she deftly moved the needles.

In the dream, he stood to the side, mesmerized by her fingers. He stepped closer, his hand drawn to the lush richness of her hair.

A smile tipped up the corner of her mouth as his heart pounded, and her hands stilled. She turned her head as his fingers sank into her hair.

The earth shifted, or a cloud moved, and the sun's glow became a harsh glare, blinding him to the beauty before him and awakening him from the familiar dream.

7

EDEN, GROWN-UP COTTON CANDY

THREE AND A HALF YEARS LATER

"Why can't she see that this guy is a loser?" Gideon grumbled.

"Because they need us to watch more episodes," I explained.

"Mission accomplished. We have seen every episode of this show at least twice!"

"Oh, are you embarrassed to be seen watching a girly show?" I teased.

"My masculinity can handle watching a show called *Village Girls*," Gideon replied drily. "Everyone here has watched it too, including Mr. Mann."

Now I was the one who felt embarrassed. Gideon was on an assignment for the family with Mr. Mann and a few others. But when time allowed, Gideon and I would often watch shows together, even though we weren't physically in the same space. I always assumed he was not with others while we watched. His camera was often off for security reasons so I could not tell. As for me, I generally watched the shows alone in my suite with him on speaker.

"Are they watching it with you now?" I asked mortified.

"No," he replied with an exaggerated sigh. "I don't watch this drivel with anyone but you. One of them saw me watching in passing, told everyone else, and now they are dropping references to the show hoping to get on my good side. They don't know I'm watching with you, except maybe Mr. Mann."

"Oh." No need to say more with Gideon.

"Exactly," Gideon replied.

"You really think it's drivel?" I said, changing the topic.

"Yes, complete drivel. She should have broken up with him a long time ago. I'm not sure how the actors can produce so many tears."

"They hold onions to their faces," I explained, while trying to think if there actually was a lot of crying in the show.

As I fast forwarded the episodes in my mind, I had to concede that Gideon was correct, there was crying in every episode. In the show *Village Girls*, the heroine spent years in a relationship with someone, thinking they would eventually get married. She was a scholarship student from the poor side of town, while he was the golden-haired, extremely wealthy, and super talented athletic soccer player. He cheated on her with her best friend. Her family blamed her for not being enough. They had been hoping she would marry the town's golden boy and bring money to the family. She eventually left her family and found a new relationship with someone who valued her. Lots of opportunities for crying and terse scenes along the way.

Gideon interrupted my musing. "I hate to cut this short, but I must prep for a meeting. I should be home in the next couple of days."

"Really?" I asked, not daring to hope. "You didn't think you would be able to get away before?"

"I can make time for what's important," he said, making me smile.

"The family will be excited to see you," I replied demurely but I could literally feel my own heart's enthusiastic pounding.

"I will be excited to see you," Gideon said, the bass timbre of his voice causing tingles to float through me like sparkling bubbly. "Our calls are not enough. I need to see you in person."

"Me too," I squeaked out. "I mean I want to see you in person."

He laughed, "I know what you meant."

There was silence for a beat and then he asked. "Do you still intend to leave the island when you graduate?"

Shocked by the question, I stammered out. "I don't know, nothing has changed, right?"

"Hasn't it?" he replied, his tone annoyed. Before I could reply he indicated that he had to go.

Dismayed at his annoyance, I conceded to myself that he made a valid point. In the last year, things had shifted. We used to talk on the phone about once a week, then twice a week, and now we were talking multiple times a day. At first, we talked more as I adjusted to being a royal ward at college. The king and queen were busy ruling and Gabriel and Lily were busy raising the twins in between royal duties. Gideon was the one who advised me on managing the pressure of attending college under constant scrutiny. It felt more like an older brother giving advice to a younger sibling. But as time passed and we talked more frequently, we shared more and more of our everyday life until nothing felt off limits. One day I had the uncomfortable realization that I no longer thought of him as my borrowed brother. Astonished at my own wayward thought, I had promptly shoved the notion away, but it kept popping up at random moments. And now, after the conversation with Gideon, it hung over my head like a cartoon bubble with a question mark. After an hour of wondering what Gideon meant, I shook my head and started planning my schedule for the week ahead.

"YOU LOOK EVEN MORE GORGEOUS!" Ya Ya cried as she clasped her hands together, her thin frame cocooned by a thick sky-blue robe held together by a yellow, almost golden belt as her long soft hair swayed gently around her face. I wished I shared her enthusiasm as I stood on the small stand for her inspection.

I looked horrible, *très terrible* in layers of pink tulle and silk cascading from my waist like a blindingly bright pink lemonade fountain. The top part was fitted with ivory silk covered with pink lace. All I needed was a red beret and I could be a human strawberry shortcake. I cringed as I saw myself from every unflattering angle in the wall-to-wall mirrors.

"Perhaps," Lily diplomatically interjected, "fewer layers?" She had not tried on her dress yet.

"It is my wedding," Ya Ya replied, her eyes narrowing as she stiffened her spine.

"Actually, Mother, it is called a renewal of vows ceremony," Queen Jasmine said as she walked into the dressing room.

I held my breath as I stood on the dais, crossing my fingers that matters would end there, but the queen's predatory smile told me she was just getting started.

"This is your third renewal ceremony in how many years?" she inquired as if she did not know the answer.

"I guess that is the difference between you and me," Ya Ya began with a deceptively sweet smile. "I celebrate every second, every minute I can be with Adam. You, on the other hand, have been married for more than twenty-five years, and you did not even have a silver wedding anniversary celebration."

"Well, I could have an anniversary celebration if . . ."

"Excuse me," Lily said apologetically as she was breaking protocol by interrupting. "I'm going to check on the girls."

I refrained from mentioning that the twins were at a birthday party outside the palace, and stepped gingerly down the steps, trying not to trip as the two elders exchanged barbs back and forth. They did not acknowledge or admonish me as I shuffled ungracefully to the changing room. An assistant rushed to aid me; I think more to prevent the dress from being torn than to help me.

"Madame has unique taste," she commented.

I said nothing in response as I had been constantly reprimanded in the past for being too friendly with the staff. Now that I was almost twenty, I had developed the habit of remaining silent when a response was not really needed.

I breathed a sigh of relief once I was back in my own clothes, a dark jean skirt with a purple Island University T-shirt and black tennis shoes.

My phone buzzed with a text from Lily. *Sorry, did you escape?*

Yep, I texted back.

Girls are back. Talk later, she wrote.

I sent her a virtual thumbs-up, but then my phone rang. It was Joannie, one of my friends from college.

Aware that my time in the Royal Family Li was limited, I had pushed myself to make friends during my first year in college, and I was pleased to end that year with a few close friends. By the end of my second year, however, I was a little less needy and more discerning.

To be honest, sometimes my friends could get on my nerves. Lizzy would get back with her boyfriend for the zillionth time; Candace would not gain a pound despite her obsession with "feeling fat;" Lilith could be somewhat unfeeling; and Joannie, well, she could talk a lot. As an experiment once, I did not cut off the conversation on the phone and inadvertently fell asleep. I woke up two hours later with Joannie still talking. Remembering that time and feeling guilty, I decided to answer the call.

"Did you hear about Jasen and Lilith?" she asked, excited.

I had heard, but I let her give a play-by-play description of Lilith's one-week relationship with Jasen. I thought Jasen was good for Lilith, or maybe I was only glad that being in a relationship made her less argumentative. I relaxed as I walked back to my suite, listening to Joannie.

"Hey, did you tell Lena she could join us for coffee tomorrow?"

"Um, no," I said. "I barely know her. She transferred in." I met Lena at the beginning of my second college year during a meet and greet for transfer students. I had volunteered for reception-table duty.

"Welcome to Island University!" I had said as I handed her a university swag bag filled with inexpensive items like small stress balls but labeled with the university's logo. There was a stillness about her that made her seem more mature than other students. I wondered if she had worked before returning to school.

"How is your family in Saved America?" she had asked. Plenty of people asked about my life in Saved America. I had grown adept at giving limited responses. Most people were just making conversation. But her question was specific to my family, asked with a small smirk playing at the corner of her mouth.

Anger popped out of the small box in which I contained it and multiplied tenfold until it filled my entire being. I held on to the reception table with gripping fingers, my tight smile seeming fake even to me.

"Thank you for your concern," I replied and dismissed her by smiling at the next student in line.

"My name is Lena," she said before walking away. We did not have much interaction after that introduction, but from time to time, I would have the sensation of being watched and would look up and see her staring. When she noticed me looking, she would give me a condescending shake of her head with a sly smile. I was determined to ignore her, but her presence made me uneasy. I thought of mentioning her to my personal guard, but there was nothing concrete to report. How do you report a feeling?

Now I wondered why Joannie mentioned her joining us for coffee.

"Why?" I asked.

"She said she would join us?" Joannie said, but it came out more like a question.

"We'll just go somewhere else," I said.

The conversation ended shortly thereafter because Joannie had to head to her summer internship. I thought over the issue with Lena. Why would she invite herself to coffee?

Hearing footsteps behind me, I did a half-turn and then a full turn as I recognized the two men. It was Gideon with Mr. Mann, my father in an earlier life. We were in the gallery with the huge windows facing the island.

"Gideon!" I exclaimed, greeting him first, noticing my father's mouth tighten, but all I could register was the tight hug from Gideon, inhaling the familiar scent of him. He was finally home.

Pulling back but still holding on to my arms, he scanned me up and down, "You totally look like a college student."

I rolled my eyes, and he laughed, the deep reverberations creating a sense of rightness when I did not even know something was off before. He was right, in person was definitely better than video.

Discomfited, I stepped out of Gideon's arms and gave a stiff perfunctory bow in response to Mr. Mann's equally perfunctory bow.

Before things could turn awkward, Gideon said, "So what color are the bridesmaid dresses this time? Orange and fuchsia?"

Now it was my turn to chuckle as Ya Ya was not known for picking the best bridesmaid dresses.

"They're pink," I said as I wrinkled my nose. "Lots and lots of pink."

Instead of laughing as I expected, Gideon gave me an intense look.

Feeling disrespectful, I backtracked. "She seems to like the color. She's knitting the girls pink hats," I mumbled, shoving my hands in the too-small pockets of my skirt.

Gideon's lips quirked up in an amused smile.

Relieved, I smiled back as our gazes locked.

"Do you know how to knit?" Mr. Mann asked.

"I'm trying to learn from Ya Ya," I said, distracted by the lingering look from Gideon.

"You'll get it," Gideon said confidently, patting me on the shoulder before apologetically excusing himself.

I stared after him, still missing hanging out with him.

"He's too familiar with you," said my father.

"He's like my brother," I retorted, frowning inwardly at the dishonesty.

He raised one of his eyebrows, his disbelief palpable.

Feeling embarrassed, I mumbled something about talking later and rushed away.

"Wait, I'll walk with you," Mr. Mann said as he jogged to catch up to me.

"Suit yourself," I muttered.

"Saved America has resumed asking for your return," he murmured in English.

"I'm almost twenty," I replied dismissively in English as well, wondering for the umpteenth time why he worried over this issue. He had successfully lobbied Gideon to advocate against my going to college in England, afraid I would be abducted and taken to Saved America.

"Do you consider yourself to be American or an islander?" he asked.

"An islander," I replied automatically, stopping abruptly as I realized the statement was true. There would be no going back for either of us.

"Your mom would be proud of you," he said. I detected a slight quaver in his voice, but his face was impassive. The plastic surgery made it difficult to tell his expression sometimes. I felt another surge of resentment as I blinked back the tears that just the thought of my mother could bring.

He continued, "It's a good quality not to be consumed by the past."

I agreed wholeheartedly. Yet why did I feel a sense of loss? I wondered if my father felt it too. While I missed the sense of security I had before I went away to high school, what I really missed was family. The Royal Family Li was a luxurious but temporary family. And the scandal a few years ago did not help matters. It all started at Gideon's grandmother's original wedding to Brother Adam.

That had been a formal affair with an elegant black-and-white color scheme, with aromatic bunches of island flowers adding splashes of color in various shades of lavender. The abundant fairy lights and real vanilla-scented candles added to the romantic ambiance, along with the Brahms-playing musicians. Over six hundred guests partook liberally from the open bars, abundant island seafood, imported beef, heart-shaped breads, and cane-sugar-laden desserts.

The king, however, had sat stone-faced throughout the entire ceremony, so the sector heads were muted in their congratulations. On the other hand, I unexpectedly found myself wiping away a tear or two as I saw the beaming faces of Ya Ya and Brother Adam.

"Are you that moved?" Gideon had asked as we sat at the family table during the reception in the palace ballroom.

"Yes," I replied. I wanted to say something about how they finally got a chance to be together, but then he might have interpreted that as a slight against his grandfather, Ya Ya's first husband.

"You want a slice of cake?" he asked, holding his dessert plate out to me. I had opted for a mixed-berry dessert, forgoing the dense, multilayered chocolate cake Gideon now held out to me. I was going to say no, but the rich, sweet smell of sugared cocoa enticed me closer, and my mouth watered in anticipation.

"Maybe we can share?" I suggested, already reaching for my fork.

"Sure," he replied. "But that means I get at least half, not a tiny bit that you leave on the plate."

"Whatever," I said right before I stuffed a large piece into my mouth. It was everything I thought it would be—dense, rich, and creamy.

I gave Gideon a thumbs-up with one hand as I used the fork to point to my mouth.

Gideon laughed, and then a flash momentarily blinded me. The wedding photographer stood there and nodded before heading off to take more photographs.

"Hopefully, that photo won't end up on *The Glitter Tattle*," Gideon said, frowning.

"Yeah," I agreed. "Eating cake is a definite scandal that should not get out at all."

Gideon and I gave each other knowing looks, and a strange sensation fluttered through me. Confused, I lowered my gaze and started to pull my hair forward but stopped midway as I remembered the torturous hours of having it straightened and artfully arranged into a complicated updo with a few tendrils spiraling down and framing my face.

Feeling a tug on one of the tendrils, I peeked up to see Gideon grinning.

"What?" I asked, suddenly irritated.

"You got chocolate on your hair," he said, half laughing.

"I didn't!" I exclaimed, grabbing my hair to inspect. He was correct; there was a square inch of hair that was glued together by cake icing. Groaning, I said, "Please tell me you didn't put it there."

Our small squabble was broken by the sound of laughter from Gabriel and Lily who sat across from us.

Gabriel mock frowned. "Lily, I thought we left the kids at home."

Lily giggled in response and swayed in her chair. She may have had one too many glasses of champagne, but it was good to see her relaxed and happy. As part of the bridal party, we both wore creamy high-necked sleeveless silk dresses that Lily had fortunately been allowed to pick out for the bridesmaids.

King Edward and Queen Jasmine were mingling with the guests, and we were all behaving less formal than usual. Feeling as though I really was drinking champagne, I twirled my champagne flute filled with apple cider and laughed at Gideon sticking his tongue out at his brother. Strange to think back on that night and realize that was the moment everything changed.

The Glitter Tattle did indeed cover Brother Adam and Ya Ya's wedding. There was the obligatory photo of the couple. Unfortunately, the photos that got the most clicks were the ones with Gideon and me. The king and queen were not amused. I was not privy to all the closed-door meetings, but the end result was that Gideon and Mr. Mann spent significantly more time abroad. When they were back on the island, Gideon would arrange for me to spend time with Mr. Mann, ostensibly to give me diplomacy lessons. These times allowed me to spend time with my father without anyone finding out about our true relationship. It also meant I saw little of Gideon.

"THIS IS NOT THE SAME DRESS," I said as I twirled around in front of the mirror. A ballerina-style dress without the poof but long in length greeted me. Most fortunately, it was in a pale, understated rose.

"I know," Lily said from the dressing room next to mine. A moment later, I heard her say, "Are you decent?"

She came into my dressing room her normal gorgeous self, only dressed as a strawberry shortcake. The extra poufy pink skirt, with pink lace over the white silk top, completed with a red beret, did look better on her than on me, but it was an extremely low bar.

"You look so lovely!" she exclaimed, turning me this way and that way, clearly pleased with how I looked.

"You look . . ." I started, not sure how to finish.

"I know what I look like," she said archly. "But at least they were able to change your dress."

"Did Ya Ya change the style again?" I asked, curious but pleased with the result.

"No, I did," Lily said with her hands on her hips. She looked around, her gaze landing on Queen Jasmine talking to a seamstress several feet away.

"Let me fix your hair," she said as she took my hand and tried to pull me closer, but I resisted turning my head to look at the mirror, touching it here and there to make sure no strands were out of place. The hairstylist had just finished working on it not more than two hours ago.

"You are so clueless," Lily said, but she was smiling as she leaned in and whispered, "Gideon is going to walk you down the aisle as part of the bridal party."

I gasped as I caught her gaze in the mirror and then slapped my hand over my mouth.

"You think you all's late night calls went unnoticed, didn't you? Try to be a little cooler during the actual ceremony." Lily smirked as she pointed at my hand still over my mouth.

"We were just catching up," I protested.

"Honey, you talk more with Gideon than I do with my own husband," Lily retorted.

That may be because your relationship is not the best, I thought, but knew better than to say that aloud.

"What about Simon?" I asked instead. He was supposed to walk with me.

"Too inebriated to walk a foot, let alone down the aisle," Lily replied. "I thought Gideon would be a better fit."

"Wait, what about . . ." I tried to think of the name of the girl who had been assigned to walk with Gideon.

"She was with Simon."

"How convenient," I murmured as I tried hard not to laugh, but a snicker did escape.

"Behave," Lily hissed, but she too was also trying not to smile.

Since I had vowed to be a proper ward for the renewal ceremony, I decided to adhere to her actual command, if not the spirit of the command. I gave her an obviously fake smile. "Yes, old and wise Older Sister."

Lily gave me an equally artificial smile. "You're welcome, Little Sister. Can you go check on the twins?"

"Twin girls or little monsters?" I asked, all wide-eyed innocence before we both started uncontrollably laughing.

"Girls!" That tone meant the queen was seconds away from losing it.

Slipping away to do as Lily had asked, I opened the door set aside for the wedding party. I saw Amara and Aditya dressed in exact replicas of my dress.

Really, Lily? I thought. *I got a kid dress?*

"Auntie Eden! Auntie Eden!" The girls jumped up before their nanny could stop them, spilling half the flower petals from their flower girl baskets.

"Girls, let's try and get these back in," I urged as I kneeled to help them.

The door opened, and there was Gideon. Of course, I was still on my hands and knees.

"Amara took more!" Aditya yelled. She had not yet discovered her "inside" voice.

"I did not!" came Amara's quieter but firm reply.

Aditya grabbed a handful from Amara's basket. "Mine," she declared.

"No, miss . . ." the nanny interjected, but by now both girls were crying, and petals were flying everywhere.

"What is the meaning of this?" Lily gasped from the doorway.

In seconds, she had the girls apologizing and picking up the petals.

Gideon and I escaped to the east garden. For the renewal ceremony, Ya Ya decided to stay at the palace, having the ceremony and early dinner in the ballroom next to the east garden. However, she wanted us to do pre-wedding pictures in the garden before the ceremony, so that was what we did. The twins and I took several pictures together in our matching dresses. The little girls' joyful smiles of anticipation at being able to participate in the ceremony chased away any minor annoyance at being dressed like a kid.

Finally, we all stood in a line: Aditya, Amara, Gabriel, Lily, Ya Ya, Brother Adam, Queen Jasmine, King Edward, Gideon, and me. As I looked down the line, I was unexpectedly filled with a feeling of longing. In a few years, would someone else be in my spot—would I be erased out of the pictures?

As we moved in line for the procession, I tried to keep smiling brightly, but Gideon leaned over slightly to ask, "What's the matter?"

"Just hoping I look okay," I whispered back.

"That's not what you're thinking," he replied. "But for the record, you look just fine."

"I look like cotton candy!" I grimaced, holding up the bouquet of pink tulips. "I should be holding up lollipops!"

"You look stunning," he said, giving me his arm. "Not the little high schooler anymore."

"I was never the little high schooler," I said as I glanced sideways at him, pleased that he thought I was stunning. I could not help the smile that spread across my face.

As we walked down the aisle, the smile became fixed as I felt everyone's gaze on us. You would think after so many vow renewal ceremonies that the guest list would shrink, but it had almost doubled from the original wedding. All the women wore some variation of pink, purple, or blue. Instructions must have been written on the invitations. The combination of the dresses and flowers in similar colors made for a kaleidoscope of colors and floral smells, making me dizzy.

I gripped Gideon's arm tighter, determined not to embarrass myself. Once we got to the minister and Brother Adam, it was a relief to be out of the spotlight. My smile became more genuine as Brother Adam watched Ya Ya walk down the aisle.

This was the first year of his married life that he was unable to do the renewal of vows ceremony standing up, so he sat upright in his new wheelchair, still snazzy in his tuxedo with a pink cummerbund, pink tie, and pink oxygen tubes to match Ya Ya's outrageously poufy dress. But on her, it worked.

As she walked, she ate up the attention, smiling and waving at her audience. I envied her confidence. I wondered how many more renewal ceremonies there would be. Here my heart froze against the unbidden thought. I shoved it promptly to the recesses of my mind and focused on the vows.

"Ya Ya, every day with you is a gift. Here I am in a wheelchair, old and can barely breathe. But every day I wake with you by my side is like my birthday and every special holiday rolled into one," Brother Adam professed, his hand clasped to Ya Ya's.

I surreptitiously wiped a tear away, only to catch Gideon's small smirk across the way. I pointedly looked away, determined not to create another "scandal."

After a long receiving line and a multi-course meal sitting between the queen and Lily, I was more than a little relieved when the dancing started. After a few obligatory dances with members of the royal family, I danced in a group with my college friends, all except Lilith who seemed glued to Jasen's side. During a break in dancing, I noticed Brother Adam moving his upper body in jerky dance moves with one of the queen's sisters. Realizing I had missed him from earlier, I went to ask Brother Adam to dance.

"My dance card is full, honey," he told me with a wink. There was actually a line, but I could see his shoulders starting to droop. He would not last another hour. I looked around for Ya Ya and saw her approaching with Gideon.

"Thanks, old man," Gideon said. "It was nice of you to hold my place in line."

"What are you talking about?" Brother Adam replied. "This line is for me." The two of them laughed as Ya Ya and I shook our heads.

Ya Ya claimed the next dance with Brother Adam, and seconds later, I was dancing with Gideon. We danced to island music, including a line dance which I had only done a few times. I missed a step, causing Gideon to miss a step, and then the whole line was out of step, causing a great deal of laughter. Finally, we all got back on the right beat and finished the song.

Then Gideon surprised me when an upbeat song came on and he

twirled me about. I laughed again as I realized my hair had become completely undone and was twirling with me. We ignored the flash of the cameras and just danced, the joy of movement and companionable company taking precedence.

But then there was a moment of too many flashes, causing my eyes to see orange and yellow. Immediately, I was jerked back into time where a fire had driven me and my friends out of the Joseph Hyde School for Exceptional Girls. I felt overheated, sweat pouring out of me, shaking as hungry flames surrounded me like a monster of old opening its prehistoric mouth wide to devour me.

"Eden," Gideon urgently whispered. "Are you with me?"

Disoriented, I slowly came to the realization of where I was. We were still dancing, but it was more of a shuffle, as Gideon held my still body closer than propriety allowed. I realized my face was wedged against his shoulder, facing away from the few media photographers who had been allowed in.

"I'm here," I mumbled.

"Let's get out of this crush," he said before taking my hand and leading me to the bar away from curious faces and the press.

I kept my head down, hoping to avoid interacting with anyone else for a moment. I hadn't taken but two steps when the twins barreled into me.

"Take a picture with us!" they demanded as they frenetically jumped up and down, their small arms held up.

A beleaguered Lily came running up. "Girls!" she said sternly. "It's your bedtime. We have to leave."

Aditya's face scrunched up in such a way that I knew she would start full-on screaming any second, and Amara's mouth was trembling. They were overstimulated and needed to rest.

"I will take one picture with you only if you go right to bed afterward," I bargained, looking at Lily to see if she agreed, but she was looking at the girls.

They nodded their heads solemnly, so we took a picture in our matching dresses. To my surprise, they actually left with Lily after we said our goodbyes. Smiling at the memory of Lily's mouthed *Thank you*, I headed to the bar with Gideon.

"You want a pink lemonade?" he asked, and I nodded my assent. He ordered seltzer water with lime for himself.

"Where were you?" he asked, and I realized he had never let go of my hand. I stared at our joined hands, fighting an urge to hold on tighter. For a teensy, tiny moment, my heart wondered at the possibilities. But then I remembered that my reality was not to be a ward or member of the royal family forever, but to make my own way.

"Eden?" he probed.

Taking my hand from his with a sigh, I took a sip of the lemonade, which, while satisfactorily cold, was overly sweet.

"I don't know," I said in a low voice, avoiding looking at him. "I was dancing, and then the next thing I knew, I was back at my high school and the fire . . ."

I stopped talking, disturbed at how my brain had put me somewhere other than reality. For a long torturous moment, I had been transported back in time to my high school, which was supposed to be a refuge but was instead a way for rich people to order fertile brides without using surrogates. Companions could also be procured for those who wanted to experience the world's oldest form of companionship. The girls being trained to be companions literally burned the school down.

"I'm so very sorry you went through that awful experience," he said, his voice filled with sadness.

I finally looked up, and my heart churned at the distress on his face.

"It wasn't all bad," I conceded. "I had Kaitlyn and Bethany." I lightly rubbed the space just above my heart, feeling the familiar ache of not knowing where they were.

"The investigation is still open, but nothing yet."

I could see how much the admission cost him by his rigid posture and his grip on his glass. He was disappointed in himself.

I reached out to touch him, to soothe him, to assure him I placed no blame. But this was not the place for that, so I let my hand drop. Instead, I said, "I am still praying. Besides, the school fund is doing some good."

The fund was started to help other Joseph Hyde School girls get a start in life through education and foster families.

He nodded as he picked up my lemonade. "You keep scrunching up your nose when you take a sip. Is it not good?"

"It has a weird taste," I shrugged.

"Your friends from college seem nice. I feel like I know them from our phone conversations." He started to take a sip but then paused and sniffed instead.

"It's lemonade, not wine," I said, thinking he should know as he'd ordered it for me.

He ignored my comment and asked a waiter for an unopened bottle of water and two fresh glasses. He then called a royal guard member over, whispering in his ear before handing him the seltzer and the mostly full glass of lemonade.

Seeing my confused face, he said, "It smelled too sweet." He then opened the bottle of water, gave me a glass, and continued, "I danced with Jeannie...no, Joannie. She can talk. I thought you were exaggerating."

"If anything, I downplayed her excessive talking," I said, noting that he was trying to look relaxed, but he really was not. He still had the frown line, and his body was still. "But there's this girl named Lena."

"What sector is she from?"

"She's a foreign student. Her name is actually something longer than Lena." I drummed my fingers against the glossy bar counter as I tried to remember her full name.

"It's Angelina!" I snapped my fingers as the name popped out. "Said she used to go by Angel in high school."

8
GIDEON, MY GIRL?

*A*t Eden's words, Gideon's overheated red blood cells froze. The glass slipped from his numb fingers, destined to crash into the unyielding marble floor and shatter into sharp glass shards mixed with spraying water and ice, but Eden gracefully leaned over and intercepted the glass mid-descent.

Her actions pulled him from his momentary shock and captured him under another spell altogether. For as she looked at him, her dark eyes wide and filled with concern for him, a sense of rightness and euphoria warmed the ice that had momentarily frozen him.

Eden was the woman of his dreams and heart. He had always been drawn to her, her wry sense of humor, her understanding of him. Their conversations over the past year had shifted his perception of her. When the line between like and love had been crossed, he did not know. When had he stopped viewing as abhorrent the idea of marrying her to appease his parents' misplaced vanity?

Her familiar face ensnared him, his captivated eyes tracking the heightened color in her cheeks and the question in her eyes. He had to consciously avoid leaning forward. Still their gazes held, carrying a silent current volleying back and forth between two willing charges. He almost raised a finger to trace her nose, a gesture that he had done flippantly before but now seemed suddenly more intimate.

Angel. Remembering the name that caused him so much heartache, he clenched his fists and looked away—straight into the face of his inebriated cousin Simon.

"Can't believe you're drinking water!" Simon scoffed before turning to his date. "I guess open bars don't mean as much when you live at the palace."

But Gideon ignored the jibe and focused on Simon's date. There was something familiar about her.

"Gideon, this is Lena. Hello, Lena," Eden greeted her, her voice subdued as her hand rubbed her throat.

Gideon felt the hairs on the back of his neck rise as he stared at the changed face of his former friend, classmate, and, to his greatest shame, lover. Suddenly, the game became clear. Eden's lemonade had been spiked with something nefarious.

Surreptitiously, while removing the glass from Eden's hand and placing it on the counter, he pressed a button on his watch phone.

Turning to Eden, his voice almost guttural, he asked, "Do you trust me?"

Eden nodded slowly as she looked between Lena and him.

Lena said nothing, just stared at him with a mocking expression. Watching while he worked it out.

Wasting no time, he grabbed Eden's hand firmly and pulled her into a half run/half walk through the crowd. He ignored the exclamations of shock that rippled through the other guests when the discreetly signaled guards surrounded them and forged a path. They raced through a blur of ornate wedding finery. His only goal was to get Eden to the infirmary before more damage was done. He wondered if running would cause the poison to move more quickly through her system. He paused, pivoted, and picked her up.

"Gideon!" she said, completely shocked.

"You said you trusted me," he gritted out as he continued moving.

"Yes, when you weren't acting—"

Her words were swallowed by a pop and then a cracking sound. Then piercing screams and confused exclamations began to fill the air and the crowd shoved against them, trying to reach the open garden doors.

Gideon's unease ratcheted up as his military experienced mind immediately characterized the sequential popping sounds as automatic gunfire. The intruders needed to be disarmed quickly and his fingers itched for a weapon, something, anything to use for defense. But then the security team encircled him and Eden again, forcing the crazed crowd back. Instead, the crowd flowed around them until another round of loud pops led to the intense screaming of the suddenly bereaved.

"On the ground! On the ground!" Lena's voice and several others were saying.

Gideon turned in horror to see blood spreading beneath several individuals who had been shot. Almost everyone was on the floor. But Gideon's unmitigated rage mixed with the worst fear at the sight of Aditya and Amara held captive by Lena, who held a firm grip on each girl's upper arm. Four large men had guns trained on the girls. Gideon resisted the temptation to look for the rest of his family. His heart trembled as he heard the wheezing Eden tried to suppress, her arms wrapped around his neck.

"Eden, Eden. Tsk, Tsk. You should have just had coffee with me," Lena said in an abnormally normal tone of voice. Gideon realized she was wearing an amplifier when he saw the wires snaking their way up from a small box at her waist to her ear. She planned this hideous violence, Gideon realized.

God help us all, he thought. Desperate to head off more bloodshed, he sank to his knees, placing Eden on the ground before slowly raising his hands.

"What do you want, Angel?" he shouted, looking for any angle to turn the tide. He heard the muffled exclamations of surprise and dismay.

The guards tightened their grips on their weapons, still standing. He knew if Angel demanded that they surrender their weapons, they would shoot. In order to save the king and Gabriel, they would sacrifice the girls. He prayed it would not come to that.

"Don't move!" Lena commanded the girls who huddled together, shaking and silently crying.

Her lithe figure moved through the groaning bodies toward Gideon, holding a gun one of her comrades had handed to her.

Crack!

A huge split opened across the ceiling, perhaps caused by one of the invaders' guns. The crack extended to the chandelier which tilted to one side with Lena standing underneath.

"Guess it's not my time to go just yet," Lena cackled as she stepped forward.

"Lena . . ." one of her men warned.

Too late. The other half of the one-and-a-half-ton chandelier broke from its mooring and plummeted towards her. Her mouth widened as she moved, but she was too slow. The chandelier slammed her to the ground, fracturing the floor and cracking and scattering the Swarovski crystals until they were drenched in Angel's blood that had exploded out of her flattened body. Gideon breathed shallowly to push back the nausea and forced himself to widen his gaze.

Two of Angel's men turned away from the twins and moved toward the fallen fixture, only to be shot through their necks by the royal guards. Their bodies jerked before falling against the chandelier.

The two remaining gunmen started to retreat but then slapped their exposed necks. As comprehension dawned, they became enraged and raised their guns again on the girls before sliding unconscious to the floor.

The girls were safe. But Gideon could neither feel relief nor focus on the grotesque scene before him of blood, bits of body parts, and dead bodies marring the clear crystal that had been mounted with such fanfare by his parents years ago. There would be no resolution between him and Angel. She was dead and he had to focus on the living.

He yelled at the guards to get the twins and medical help as he felt for Eden's pulse. It was very faint.

As the royal guards moved to disarm the unconscious men, medical personnel rushed in with worried faces, coming directly to him and Eden but focusing on him.

He slapped their probing hands away, barking at them to "Save Eden! She's been poisoned!" Ignoring the crunch of broken crystal beneath his feet, he then ran to his nieces, who were surrounded by royal guards, but his brother arrived at the same time.

"Daddy!" they cried as they clung to their father, their arms a vise around his neck.

Gideon hurried back to Eden. He held his breath as they inspected her, cataloging areas of concern as they moved in a flurry of activity. A breathing mask was put over her face and an IV in her arm before they loaded her on a gurney.

"Sir," the senior doctor said, turning to him. "She will be taken to the hospital, not the infirmary."

"Will she recover?" he asked, bracing himself for the response.

"I'm not sure, but I would say she has a better chance than the others," the doctor replied before flicking her gaze over those on the floor being checked by other medical staff. It was obvious to all that their prognosis was not so good.

As he watched Eden being wheeled out, the king rushed into the room and ran over, grabbing him into a firm embrace. He finally released his son but kept a grip on his arm, inspecting him up and down. "Are you hurt anywhere?"

Gideon shook his head. "Is everyone okay?"

"Your tip to the guards helped them extract us before Angel and her team could take over the ballroom."

"Eden and I were on the opposite side," Gideon noted.

"I know," his father said, scanning the room. The royal guards were interviewing guests and keeping the chaos organized while medical personnel tried desperately to save the wounded.

His father continued, "I watched it all unfold in the situation room with your brother. He slipped out while I was talking to someone else, to get to the balcony. He shot the darts at the last two of Angel's men."

"Keeping them alive helps for interrogation purposes," Gideon conceded as a group of medical personnel ran out holding up a stretcher.

His father gave Gideon's arm another brief squeeze before releasing him, and they turned their attention to comforting the grieving.

AFTER HE RECEIVED confirmation that the families of the deceased had been notified, Gideon walked outside to the east garden. Dawn was breaking. The breathtaking sight of the sun's rays dispelling the evening's darkness made his heart ache with grief. The sun could not bring back the dead nor return the time that had passed. He sat on the ground and wept for what was lost.

He had intended to stay out in the garden for a short time, understanding that the crisis was not yet over. But weary from grief and lack of sleep, his body was dragged into an uncomfortable rest.

A mild kick to his leg woke him. Squinting, he saw his brother and moved to get up, but Gabriel waved him off and sat down, handing him a cup filled with aromatic dark coffee.

Gideon gratefully accepted the coffee, gulping a caffeine-laden swallow. "What time is it?" he asked.

"Ten," his brother replied.

"What?" He sat straight up, horrified.

His brother held up his hand. "We have a few minutes to have coffee," he wrinkled his nose, "and to take a shower."

Gideon raised his arm to smell himself and recoiled. "Not the worst I've smelled, but I definitely need a shower."

Gabriel shook his head, and the brothers sat in silence a minute more as the sun blazed a brighter golden hue against the blue sky.

"Last night . . ." Gideon began but stopped as Gabriel had started speaking as well.

"Lily wants to leave me," his brother stated, staring at the cup in his hands.

"What!" Gideon exclaimed.

"Last night, when I took the girls to Lily, Mother made one of her comments," Gideon explained.

"What did she say?" Gideon reluctantly asked.

"'It's a poor excuse of a mother, who would leave her children behind while she escaped.'"

Gideon gasped at the cruelty. "Mother said that? Those exact words?"

Gabe nodded, his face flushed red.

"I can't—I don't know what to say," Gideon said, struggling to reconcile his love for his mother with her ugly words. "Did you talk with Mother?"

Gabriel shook his head, his head bowed low.

Gideon reached out and briefly squeezed his brother's shoulder, thinking of the twins. "Wait, I saw Lily leave with the twins. How did they get back into the ballroom?"

"That's the funny part," Gabe replied in a tone that let Gideon know what he was about to say was the opposite of funny. "Lily did take the girls out. It was way past their bedtime. The nanny met her halfway, and Lily returned to the ballroom."

"Then how. . ." Gideon began.

"The nanny was stopped on the way to the girls' room by Mother, who gave in to the girls' plea to have a particular cookie from the ballroom. She told the nanny to come back in fifteen minutes and then gave the girls permission to go back to the ballroom for the cookies."

Gideon groaned in recognition. "I know which cookies. They were shaped in a bow, strawberry glaze over a thin chocolate-wafer type of cookie?"

His brother nodded.

"Did the nanny come back?" Gideon asked.

Silence greeted this question. Looking gingerly at his brother, Gideon was startled by the sight of tears running down his brother's face.

This time he reached for his brother's shoulder and held on. "Was she one of . . . was she one of the victims?"

His brother's crumpled face confirmed what Gideon dreadfully suspected.

"I'm very sorry, Gabe." Guilt weighed on Gideon as he thought of how little attention he paid to the nannies. He did not want to be the creepy guy checking out the nannies, but he could have paid more attention considering they were taking care of his nieces.

Gabe continued, "Her name was Nathalia. The girls were gorging themselves on cookies, cakes, and whatever they could get their hands on. They had hidden under one of the pastry tables. Nathalia came back as we were being hustled out, but we didn't see her. She was walking around looking for the twins when the first shot rang out."

Gideon cursed. "Does Lily blame you?"

Gabe shook his head. "She blames me for not sticking up for her when Mother attacked her."

At Gideon's questioning look, Gabe continued, "I was in shock, and then I did speak up, but Lily was already striding away with the girls." He put the coffee cup down and fisted his hands. "Amara asked Lily why she left them."

Footsteps interrupted Gideon's reply.

Gabe's assistant came upon them. Looking at their faces, he grimaced. "Shall I tell the king's staffer that you'll be ready for the debriefing in about ninety minutes?"

Gabe indicated his acquiescence to the plan.

Gideon waited until the aide was out of earshot. "Are the girls okay now?"

"No," Gabe replied. "They'll have nightmares for a while. We did our best to reassure them that we did not purposely leave them. But every-thing else will still be work for us all to get through."

"Don't they know that you didn't know—"

"But their grandmother is the one saying we left them," Gabriel interjected.

"She's deflecting from her own guilt in the situation!" Gideon exclaimed.

"I know, I know!" Gabriel agreed. "But I don't want to badmouth our mother to my children either."

"But your wife is fair game?" Gideon asked. At Gabriel's stricken look, he thought he had gone too far. "Look—"

"No, you're right," Gabriel said. "I should have said something sooner." Sighing, he stood up.

Gideon stood as well. He rubbed his hand nervously against his leg.

"About Angel..." he started.

Gabe jumped in and said, "Do not even think about apologizing for that woman."

"But... "

"But nothing," Gabe said as he grasped Gideon by the shoulder. "Whatever debt was owed, consider it paid. You cannot take responsibility for someone who starts murdering people to get her way."

The brothers hugged each other tightly before going in to face a long day of debriefings, press conferences, and hospital visits. The visits to the bereaved would be scheduled for another day.

HOURS LATER, Gideon walked with his eyes straight ahead. His gaze did not take in the medical staff moving quickly, their hurried bowing as he passed. Nor did he feel soothed by the cheery signs and strategically placed plants. Instead, he felt agitated by the scents of antiseptic and illness. Scents that no hospital could completely erase, royal wing or not.

All day he had felt pressure building within him. Debriefing, walking step by step through what happened, had made him want to punch something. He then robotically read the press statement put before him, striving to keep his voice calm. In truth, he wanted to rage and weep simultaneously.

Instead, he had splashed chilled water on his face and went with his brother to the hospital to visit a few of the survivors. Out of eleven hundred eighty-eight wedding guests, four hundred and six had been wounded, some critically, and thirty-two were dead. The wounded survivors' welcome of him felt wrong when he was the catalyst that lit the match for Angel's murderous tendencies.

"Sir, we're here," said one of the hospital's executives.

Gideon stopped, waiting for the man to open the door. Instead, the door opened from within, and Dr. Brown, Eden's doctor in London, stepped out.

Startled, Gideon took a step back. "What are you doing here?"

"I was called in to consult," the doctor said, holding the door open. "She's awake if you would like to visit."

Gideon gave a barely perceptible nod, his mind racing. Why was Dr. Brown in the royal hospital wing? How did she get clearance? What had she told Eden?

"Gideon!"

He looked past the doctor and saw Eden standing there, smiling a bit wanly but overall looking whole and healthy. Her skin had lost the unnatural hue from last night, her eyes were clear, and her hair was freshly washed. A towel was around her shoulder to protect her hospital gown from her wet hair. She must have just gotten out of the shower.

His knees almost buckled with relief at the sight of her. Instead, he went to her and pulled her into a warm hug. He could not speak past the lump in his throat, so he pulled her tighter.

She hugged him in return before gently patting his back.

"I heard about the people who died," she whispered softly. "I've been praying for their families, you, everyone."

Touched by her words but cognizant of where they were, Gideon stepped back, his hands pausing on her shoulders before forcing himself to step away and stand by her side. His entire left side felt like a magnet drawn to her.

Ruthlessly, he gripped his hands behind his back and looked around. Expecting an entire medical team, he was surprised to see only Dr. Brown and another doctor who looked vaguely familiar. Both doctors gave him tight smiles. Deeper lines fanned out from Dr. Brown's tired eyes. The other doctor had dark circles under his eyes, but there was curiosity in his gaze as he looked from Dr. Brown to Gideon.

"Dr. Brown and I have met before. Who are you?" Gideon asked brusquely, his stiff demeanor hiding the fear for Eden that gripped his heart. Was her healthy image a mirage?

The male doctor flushed red. "I'm Dr. Patel."

"Tell me what's wrong with Eden, and speak comfortably please," Gideon said.

"Gideon!" Eden interrupted, her hand touching his arm. "There's nothing wrong and stop barking orders."

"Eden is fine," Dr. Patel said. "Your guards told us what you suspected, and we were able to consult with Dr. Brown on how to treat her. She has dealt with—uh—similar cases in Untouchable City in Saved America."

Dr. Patel avoided his gaze, probably afraid he would object to a doctor from Untouchable City. But before Gideon could theoretically object, Dr. Brown continued the explanations. "We strongly suspect that Eden was poisoned with the same substance you were, years ago as a little boy."

"I was never poisoned," Gideon said, puzzled.

Dr. Patel nodded. "We thought then that it was an allergic reaction to something, but you tested negative on all the tests we gave you. Now we know more. The substance is considered poisonous for humans, not an allergen. Even though the symptoms and—"

Gideon snapped his fingers as a lightbulb went off in his head. "Ah! Dr. Patel, you were on the team of doctors who treated me."

The doctor nodded and smiled. "It's been over twenty years. I looked a lot younger then."

"Did you save the substance from before?" Gideon asked.

"We did," Dr. Patel confirmed with a frown. "The sample we saved has disappeared, and the video feed to the lab was erased."

Gideon lifted his eyes to the ceiling and counted to three. He was going for ten, but three seconds would do.

"Does anyone else know about the poison?" he asked.

The doctors looked at each other before Dr. Patel answered, "We don't know. We suspect that a few cases in Untouchable City and elsewhere may have been poisonings from the substance, but without testing and records, it's difficult to confirm."

"But you said you know what the substance is?" Gideon countered.

Dr. Patel looked at Dr. Brown, who explained. "The substance, *Inobservabilis Venenum*, is a manufactured poison made of various components of plants, one of which is a hybrid plant that grows on Mars."

"But they're not really hybrid, right?" Eden asked, looking to Gideon before turning back to the doctors. "They're Earth plants that were replanted on Mars and turned into something else entirely?"

"Correct," Dr. Brown said with a small smile. "During the unsuccessful colonization attempt, Mars became overrun with poisonous plants. No one is supposed to collect samples from the planet because of the fear of bringing back something too poisonous to contain."

"But someone did," Gideon interjected harshly.

"Yes," the doctor replied, her shoulders slumping. "The only good thing is that we know how to test for it."

"Why are the other plants needed to make the poison if the hybrid plant is so potent?" Eden asked.

"It's too unstable by itself. It needs the other plants to keep its original properties intact," the doctor replied.

I'm like the hybrid, Gideon thought to himself. *Unstable and in need of love to keep me stable.* Shaking his head at the maudlin direction his tiredness had taken him, Gideon excused himself to step into the washroom.

Once inside the washroom, he splashed water on his face and looked disparagingly in the mirror, rubbing his hand over the stubble on his chin. He itched to ditch his tie and other constrictive clothing for something more comfortable, but he still had matters to address. He needed to check on Brother Adam and Ya Ya who had also been brought to the hospital. And inform his father and Gabriel of this new poison issue. They needed to work with other countries to mitigate the risk from the poison. How had Angel gotten her hands on something so dangerous? Who added the poison to Eden's lemonade? Angel must have had a person working on the inside. With a sigh, he reached for his phone.

After a brief conversation updating his father, he opened the private washroom to step back into Eden's room. The doctors had left. Eden was sleeping on her side, facing away from him.

Suppressing an urge to twirl a curly lock of hair around his fingers, he looked around for something on which to leave her a note. Her watch phone was being held for forensic evidence.

Feeling a buzzing around his wrist, he gave up on the note and reached out to give her a quick pat on the head before leaving, but at that exact moment, she turned toward him, and his hand slid over her cheek.

Her eyes opened, and they stared at each other. He held his breath, but she only smiled, put her hand over his on her cheek, and fell back asleep.

Comfortable with her holding on to his hand holding onto her, he checked the message. It was not urgent, so he closed his eyes for a moment of respite.

9
EDEN, REALITY DREAMS

*M*y sleep-drugged eyes slid open to see Gideon leaning over me. My heart, unrestrained by partial consciousness, leapt at the sight of him, flying as sure as an eagle in flight. I turned toward him, feeling his hand whispering past my cheek as I moved. I placed my hand over his just as unsurely. The eagle within me landed hard as my eyes took in the deeper lines around his eyes and mouth, his face a tangle of hard edges. Sorrow and weariness hugged his shoulders. My hand tightened over his as I sought to both comfort him and fight off the sleep that tugged me closer to the edge of oblivion.

But soundlessly the door opened, and a slew of entertainment news hosts came marching in, their well-coiffed heads oversized and jingling side to side like church bells, not quite connecting to their stick figures. By stick, I do not mean slim or thin, I mean stick like a children's drawing.

Puzzled, I tried to put the right head with the correct stick figure, but then they stopped in a line in front of me and turned sharply, grinning maniacally as they shook their heads back and forth, mimicking their wagging figures.

Terrified, I forced my feet to move, only to be stopped by hands gripping my right shoulder. I opened my mouth to scream but came awake instead.

The first thing I noticed was the sun and the quiet. The second thing I noticed was Gideon, whose head was a dead weight against my upper arm, and whose hand held mine. The third thing I noticed was James and Luke guarding the door.

"You want to wake Sleeping Beauty?" Luke asked, his voice as sarcastic as usual.

Feeling my face redden, I wondered for the thousandth time how he stayed employed by the royal family.

"Gideon," I whispered, but he did not respond. Gently, I wiggled my arm underneath his head.

"Tell Luke I'm awake," Gideon rasped, his gravelly voice a rough caress against the silk fabric of my pajama top.

Luke rolled his eyes, but James interrupted whatever inappropriate comment was likely to come. "His change of clothes is in the washroom. He is expected at the palace."

Gideon sat up with a yawn, his hand still clasping mine. "Give me fifteen minutes," he said.

James and Luke nodded, but Gideon stared at them. They stared back with Luke raising his eyebrow. Finally, with a muffled huffing sound from Luke and a frown from James, they left.

Gideon patted my head with his free hand.

"We need to talk," he said.

The warmth I felt from his intense gaze warred with my annoyance.

"Am I a dog?" I asked.

"What?" he asked, confused.

"Why do you pat me on the head like I'm a dog?" I asked.

He leaned even closer until our faces were only inches apart.

I knew I should probably lean back, but my heart fluttered like a swarm of bees finding leftover honey within the sullen remains of a long-finished picnic, and I leaned infinitesimally closer.

A rush of victory flooded me as Gideon's lips brushed against mine, a tentative, questioning foray, before his lips pressed more firmly against mine. Excitement skittered through me like champagne bubbles as my lips arched upward into a smile. I felt his lips do the same.

He pulled back slightly, his eyes darker than usual.

"I don't think you're a dog," he whispered.

"Thanks," I whispered back, lamely. Suddenly, my brand-new, still raw emotions overwhelmed me. Embarrassed, I dropped my gaze and turned my head away, only to feel him squeeze my hand that was still captured by his.

I lifted my gaze to his, relaxing at the gentleness and acceptance I saw reflected. His hand tightened on mine as he used his other hand to cradle the side of my face, brushing my cheek with his thumb. With a muffled sigh, he pulled me to him and hugged me.

Just as I started to hug him back, he jerked away.

I blinked, confused as Dr. Brown came back in with some other medical staff. They bowed slightly toward Gideon, who with an impassive face nodded briefly in return and promptly disappeared into the washroom. The medical staff started conferring together. I heard my name a few times, but no one spoke directly to me.

Feeling overheated and off-kilter, I fanned myself with one hand as I used the remote to make a breakfast selection. Unfortunately, when I turned on the screen, the hosts from the *Glitter Tattle* came on. I learned that I was a gold-digging scammer who was planted by the American government to bring down the royal family. Gideon traveled a lot due to my inappropriate advances.

"I turned that off earlier," Dr. Brown said. "It seemed to make you restless."

I realized I must not have been fully asleep then, as the show's hosts seemed to have infiltrated my hazy consciousness to reside in my dreams.

I nodded to show I had heard Dr. Brown, but my face felt unbearably hot. I placed my hands on the sides of my face, my eyes closed, as I tried to compose myself in front of the medical staff.

As I processed the events of the past minutes, I heard bells and dings going off, and I opened my eyes. All the doctors except Dr. Brown were looking at their devices. Dr. Brown came over and placed her hand on my forehead.

"The patient is right in front of you," she sharply reprimanded the younger doctors.

They all nodded sheepishly as Gideon came out of the washroom buttoning his cuff links. With his hair still damp and his crisp white shirt well-tailored to his athletic physique, he looked very male and handsome. I squelched my annoyance when James rushed back in with Luke.

"What's going on? Where's Dr. Patel?" Gideon demanded, pointing at the medical staff before turning to the visiting doctor.

"Dr. Patel will be back later this evening," Dr. Brown replied before whispering something to the other medical staff, who shuffled out while she continued to examine me. She checked my heart rate, pulse, blood pressure, and temperature before using her hands to check under my neck and armpits.

Throughout her examination, James, Luke, and Gideon stared at me like I was a specimen in a jar. As I sat, the *Glitter Tattle's* host's words seemed to slither in and shame me. Was I too forward with Gideon? Were people judging me? I forced myself to breathe, not wanting to embarrass myself further by hyperventilating. Still, my face felt hot, and I knew my cheeks were red. I could hear the little dings being made by the medical equipment in the room.

"Is anything wrong?" Gideon finally asked, moving closer and placing his hand on my shoulder.

I looked up at him, and he gave me a smile before looking across me at the doctor. Discombobulated, I also turned toward the doctor, who stood on the other side of me. Her frown deepened as she took in Gideon's hand.

"She is very healthy," she responded. "Almost completely recovered from . . . from what happened in the ballroom."

"But you looked concerned?" Gideon pressed.

"Hmmm, I was initially," the doctor replied. "Her heart rate and blood pressure were up. But then I realized that her condition was quite common for young people who engage in prolonged kissing."

I gasped and looked at Gideon, who seemed puzzled. "Prolonged?" he asked. He was not embarrassed at all.

"Who was she kissing?" Luke asked, and James elbowed him in the side.

"Wait . . . her and Gideon?" Luke asked, his voice and eyebrows rising.

I wanted to slide under the covers.

"Everyone keep this quiet until I have a chance to talk to the palace," Gideon ordered.

"Of course, sir," James replied.

"Wh-what?" I stuttered. Things were moving too fast. We'd originally agreed not to have a relationship, thwarting his parents' plan for us. At some point, I would stop being a ward of the Royal Family Li and I would make my own way in the world. But then we'd become friends, and sometimes it would seem like we were on the cusp of something more. But nothing really changed. Well, until today.

"And Eden and I have a chance to talk," Gideon amended.

Gideon's, Luke's, and James's watch phones went off simultaneously.

Gideon sighed. "I need to take care of some things."

"Wait," I said. "How are Ya Ya and Brother Adam? Well?"

Gideon sat on the side of my bed, taking both of my hands in his before leaning in to kiss my forehead.

"I'll swing by later," he promised. "Let me get more information."

He stood and moved toward the door but paused and looked between the doctor and me, frowning.

"The resemblance is quite strong, sir," James said as he looked at the floor and then the wall.

"I can see that!" Gideon snapped. His watch phone beeped again. He swore and looked at the doctor. "Later."

She pressed her lips together but reluctantly nodded.

Gideon then gave me a tight smile and rushed out.

Just as the door closed behind James and Luke, I burst out with questions. "What was that about? What resemblance . . ."

The doctor's face shuttered closed.

"Oh, am I too young to know?" I asked, using my fingers to emphasize the quotations.

The doctor's face became amused as she fluffed the pillows behind me. "You're a grown woman, and they should treat you as such?" she asked.

"Yes, you get it," I responded, reluctantly folding my arms across my chest, wondering what smart quip I would be subject to in return.

"Well, I thought he was treating you like an adult." She smiled and winked at me as she pressed a button on her notepad.

I laughed in between stuttering out, "Well, he took me by surprise."

"Did you not consent?" she asked with a frown, putting the notepad in her pocket.

"I totally consented," I responded in surprise. "Could you not tell?"

"I . . . uh," the doctor tried to formulate a response as I realized the inappropriateness of my question.

"Never mind," I quickly said. "What's the resemblance thing they were talking about?"

"You'll have to ask him," she replied indifferently, but I saw her hands shake before she shoved them into the pockets of her white doctor's coat. I remembered the odd moments in our prior encounters.

"But you know," I inquired quietly.

"Yes," she replied just as quietly.

The door opened, but the doctor shooed away whoever it was. She turned to me; her face mired in indecision.

Encouraged, I leaned forward, my hand reaching out to her, but she stepped back.

Any discomfiture I felt at her actions was obliterated by the sight of Ya Ya being wheeled into my room.

"Ya Ya!" I exclaimed as I scrambled out of bed.

The hospital aide explained that she had asked to see me. But when I stood in front of her, I flinched. Gone was the mother of the king, the joyful later-in-life bride, and my friend who gave me unorthodox advice in between encouraging me to eat. In her place was a small, shrunken woman with grief bending her back and cruelly lining her face.

My feet itched to step back in time, into a yesterday of gentle hugs and unrestrained laughter. But what is joy without grief?

Somehow, I stumbled forward on legs that felt like jelly that had been taken out of the refrigerator too soon. I knelt before Ya Ya and took her hands in mine, almost wincing at their fragility.

"It's Brother Adam? Is he gone?" I asked softly.

She nodded blankly, tears running unheeded down her cheeks.

I heard a small noise and saw that Dr. Brown had placed a box of tissues near me. I looked up to say thanks, but she was already headed to the door, taking with her the medical person who had wheeled Ya Ya into the hospital room.

Grateful for the privacy, I turned my attention back to Ya Ya, carefully dabbing her face with the soft tissue, feeling grief well within me for Brother Adam and Ya Ya. Why was their story so short?

Ya Ya's hair hung limply, unwashed and uncombed. *Someone should have done her hair*, I thought in a random burst of anger. I wildly thought that someone should be with her, and I searched my brain for that someone. But every member of the royal family must be busy addressing the attack at the palace by Angel and her friends. I was here, so now I was that someone.

I swallowed hard as I gripped her hands. Ya Ya and I sat in silence. Time seemed without meaning in the space we shared. I could hear footsteps passing outside, and I could feel the air get hotter within the room as the sun continued to rise. The weight of grief grew heavier with each passing moment.

After a time, Ya Ya's hands went slack in mine. I wearily rose to my feet, taking the opportunity to stretch before I wheeled Ya Ya back to her room. I found it disquieting that no one else was around, especially her immediate family. I would take her to her room and track down Gideon.

But my arms paused just before they reached all the way up in my stretch, and I noticed a different type of stillness in the room. Slowly, I turned my head to look again at Ya Ya, and I waited for her chest to rise. But it didn't. Blood rushed from my head, and I stumbled, lightheaded.

"Lord, help us," I whispered as I pressed the call button frantically for help, wondering how many seconds it had been and if I should do CPR. I did not have to worry about the latter because guards and medical staff immediately entered.

I stood frozen as they frantically worked on her. And then I felt her presence enveloping me in the most loving hug. Then the presence moved on, and I realized her soul was leaving every earth-bound care behind.

Desperate, I reached out as if I alone could hold on to her soul, but of course my hands came up empty. She was gone.

I turned back to her body, which was now only a shell without a soul. A doctor knelt on either side of her body, pumping her chest to stimulate a heartbeat that would never return. They rushed her out. Who knew grief could cut like a well-sharpened knife?

Dr. Brown ran in and hugged me tightly.

Grateful for the comfort, I hugged her back.

We were facing the mirror on the outside of the washroom door, and after so many tears fell that I became dehydrated is when the picture came into focus. I finally noticed the similarly shaped noses, the almost identical full mouth, and the different-shaped eyes but with the same amber flecks visible in just the right light. Her skin tone was a deeper brown than mine, and her hair was both darker and straighter than mine. But the resemblance was unmistakable.

Like photos in a slide show, I remembered Dr. Brown's reaction to my birth date, her desire to keep me in England. Most of all, I remembered my father telling me that my birth parents were not actually dead. I did not care at the time.

But now I was curious. Was the woman embracing me my biological mother, or an aunt or even a sister?

My eyes met hers in the mirror, and I knew that she knew I knew something. I bit my bottom lip as I struggled for something to say, but it was like cotton filled my head and mouth.

We both saw the door to the room open from the mirror and took a step away from each other to face Gideon. Despite everything, the sight of him loosened the grief gripping my heart.

"That's my job," he said as he strode across the room and pulled me into a hug.

I saw a woman I didn't recognize behind him and the doctor's raised eyebrows before his broad shoulders blocked my view. I hugged him like he was a lifeline pulling me from a restless sea with a vicious undertow.

Gideon pulled me even tighter for a moment before releasing me, his hands holding mine. I frowned as I saw his eyes were full of unshed tears. I should have been comforting him. But I couldn't be that forward with the doctor still there in the room, along with the strange woman.

"We'll have to talk later," Gideon said regretfully as he let go of my hands. "Sabina will get you ready. We only have fifteen minutes."

I nodded, resigned. I had been part of the royal family long enough to know that every moment, whether happy or sad, had to have the right image. So, I subjected myself to Sabina's expertise, and fifteen minutes later, an ice maiden stood in my place. No evidence of tears, wild hair, or the foul smell of recent death remained.

Instead, a smooth natural-looking mask had been sculpted from limited edition makeup, my hair had been pulled back so tightly that no wayward curl escaped, and I had been spritzed with a light floral scent after the shortest shower in history. The dress was understated and black.

At the knock at the door, Dr. Brown, who had watched everything but the shower with worried eyes, hurriedly laid a hand on my arm. "If you ever want to make a turn from this road, a door will always be open."

I just shook my head as Gideon entered and took my hand.

We walked into a hallway lined with medical staff in utter silence, the only sound our own footsteps on the hard floor and random beeping.

Finally, we entered Ya Ya's hospital room. She was surrounded by her family: the king, her brothers Michael and Joseph, the queen, her grandsons, Lily, and me.

The medical staff began shutting down the machines one by one. Her body exhaled one last horrific mechanical breath and then lay still.

10

GIDEON, DEATH IS HARD

Gideon had never been able to accept death. Not even in the military where it was often unavoidable. He had been chosen a few times to serve on the Guard of Honor. He'd followed standard procedure, saluting the flag-draped coffin while wearing his dress uniform with the ceremonial sword. But the grief of a fallen soldier's family served as the actual weapon which cut his unsteady emotions into a thousand pieces of chaos. It was with great effort that he had stood steady and implacable.

The last time he served on the Guard of Honor, he had spent the entire night in the chapel, so great was the temptation to seek solace in a bottle. The chaplain had nodded at him in surprise when he came in. He did not speak, but Gideon had never been asked to serve in that capacity again. He felt this lack of confidence in him as a mark of shame.

He was determined to handle his beloved grandmother's death with honor. However, despite his firm determination, his heart seized at seeing her death, seeing her take those last few mechanical breaths in a diminished body. His father's weeping fractured Gideon to tears, and consistent with custom, he moved to stand with his back to his father. Gabriel did the same. Luke and James left the room. The medical staff had already left. They all acted to give the king the ability to grieve as a son whose mother had died.

Lily and Eden remained, standing on the other side of the room. Gideon wanted desperately to have Eden by his side, but Lily was crying and shaking her head as she gazed at Ya Ya's covered form. Eden had an arm around Lily's shoulders as she tried to comfort her.

A verse that Brother Adam shared with him when he was annoyed with Gabe came to his mind.

"A friend loveth at all times, And a brother is born for adversity." (Proverbs 17:17 KJV)

Thinking of Brother Adam made him remember his death and the deaths of all those for whom services were still to be held. The weight of mourning pressed him with a force he could barely withstand. He swayed as his eyes momentarily caught Eden's. She gave him a sympathetic smile before closing her eyes, and he knew she was praying for him. When she opened her warm eyes again, he mouthed, *Thank you.*

Unfortunately, his mother who was kneeling next to his father chose that moment to notice the rest of the room.

"Have you girls no shame?" she lashed out viciously. "Face the wall!"

At Eden's justifiably stunned expression, Gabe hurried to explain the tradition of facing away from a grieving king.

"I did not know," Lily whispered, her expression apologetic.

Just then, a sound came from the corpse between them.

"What?" the queen exclaimed.

"Dead bodies continue to expel gas and other . . . things," Lily gritted out.

At that moment, a foul odor filled the air.

"Get out!" the king roared.

Gideon scurried out right behind Gabriel, Lily, and Eden. As he closed the door behind him, he heard a click and looked up to see a photographer taking pictures of the family. Enraged but trying not to let it show, he stood still as his brother ushered Lily and Eden into the room next door to his grandmother's. All the while, the rogue photographer greedily took pictures, his tongue licking his lips in unholy excitement.

As soon as Gabriel returned, he exchanged a look of understanding with Gideon. This incident was not the first time they had dealt with aggressive photographers. Gideon walked away as Gabriel stayed behind, seemingly oblivious of the photographer.

"I can't believe your guards are nowhere around," the photographer said to Gabriel in a singsong voice, his expression smug as he continued snapping. "By the way, you guys owe me for the drone. They cost a lot in Saved America; you know?"

Gideon paused in his steps, wanting so badly to just pulverize the camera and the man he now knew was responsible for the incident in Saved America. But he understood that the photographer was baiting them, so he kept walking, hoping the other man stayed right where he was. He got his wish as he circled back around until he was right behind the photographer who didn't appear to hear Gideon approach.

"It's time for you to leave," Gideon said harshly.

"You gonna make me?" The photographer turned to Gideon; his face scornful.

"I won't have to," Gideon replied, purposely not looking at Gabriel, who had moved stealthily close to the man from the front. Gideon himself moved deeper into the photographer's personal space on purpose in order to keep the man distracted. "You will do it for me," Gideon said with a smirk.

The photographer replied, "Because you are a pr—what the . . ." the man sputtered as his camera was pulled hard from his hands before falling to the floor and breaking into many pieces. Gideon allowed himself a tiny smile as he saw the memory card in the debris near his foot and deliberately stepped on it. Gideon and his brother watched impassively as the man knelt on the floor with jerky movements.

"Where is it? Where is it?" the photographer muttered repeatedly to himself as he frantically searched through the pieces.

"You seem to be missing the memory card?" Gideon asked in a singsong voice of his own as he leaned sideways against the wall, his foot firmly on said memory card.

Prince Gabriel made a surprised noise. "I would have thought Drone Man would be more professional."

With a yell, the photographer raised his fist back as though to punch Gideon, who only raised an eyebrow as the guard he had discreetly summoned came running up to grab the photographer's arm and twisted it behind his back as the subdued man issued a string of curse words.

"Assaulting a member of the royal family is a crime, sir," the guard admonished.

Gideon and Gabriel watched as the guard led the sputtering photographer away. They made sure the memory card was destroyed before joining Lily and Eden again.

WHEN THE SUN rose the next morning, Gideon remembered the sweetness of Eden's kiss and the sadness of Ya Ya's and Brother Adams's deaths. Deciding he would skip his swim and have time for tea with Eden before another difficult day began in earnest, Gideon hurried through his morning ablutions and walked quickly to Eden's suite. He arrived at her door at the same time as Mrs. Wright. She gave him a slight bow, and he raised his eyebrow in inquiry.

"I'm here to help Eden understand funeral rites on the island," she said, but her eyes darted sideways, and she seemed to be pausing.

"And?" he prompted.

"And the queen thought Eden should be chaperoned during her times with you. I'm the chaperone." Mrs. Wright gave him a smug smile as she stood even straighter. Unfortunately, her smile was like a sharp pin puncturing an overinflated balloon.

Out of patience with his mom, Mrs. Wright, and the world in general, Gideon growled out, "We are way too old to need chaperones. I will speak to my mother." Then he waited to see if Mrs. Wright would challenge his authority in the name of the queen. His wish was granted when she opened and then closed her mouth like a gasping fish on dry land before bowing and scurrying away.

Still annoyed, Gideon tried to calm himself before knocking on Eden's door, but then the lady herself opened the door. Her eyes widened at the sight of Gideon.

"Gideon! I was just going to find you," she exclaimed.

"What is it?" he asked as he allowed her to lead him by the hand into her suite.

Eden started to speak but then frowned. "What were you coming to see me about?"

"This," he replied as he pulled her into his arms for a hug. He loved the way she relaxed against him, her arms rising to hold him as well. Pleased by her response to him, he held her tighter still, burying his face in her soft, fragrant hair.

After a moment, she took a step back, her hands resting on his arms which still held her. There was a question in her eyes.

"Shall we date?" he asked, his voice lower than usual.

She nodded with a small smile. He grinned back as his hand reached out to caress her cheek. The air became charged as they stared at each other with stirrings of desire. He leaned toward her and kissed her forehead before moving farther away to sit in one of her two armchairs.

"It seems we do need a chaperone," he said ruefully, running his fingers through his already tousled hair.

"Is that how we are supposed to do things?" Eden asked with a worried frown as she took the other chair.

"On the island, different families do things differently," Gideon replied with a small shrug. "But for the royal family, the brides are supposed to be above reproach."

At Eden's horrified expression, he rushed to explain, "Not that there is any question with you."

Eden stared at him with a tiny head tilt before she took a deep breath. "Gideon, what you just said was awful."

"What?" Gideon was taken aback.

"You have *carte blanche* to do whatever with whomever, yet you would bear no responsibility, only the girl you were with?" Eden couldn't keep her anger from seeping into her voice.

Gideon felt the cut of her anger rub against his slumbering guilt, and he lashed out, "What do you know about relationships that you didn't learn from watching some TV drama?"

"Better than someone whose dates are never seen in the daylight hours." Eden leaped up, equally mad.

Gideon stormed out and slammed the door. He walked away for a few steps before pivoting and returning to stare at the door. How had a simple desire to hug Eden gone so wrong? After a moment, he knocked on the door.

Eden opened the door. He could see tears glistening in her eyes.

"I'm so sorry. Can we start over?"

At her small nod and step back, Gideon came back into her suite and took both of her hands in his.

"I have a confession to make. I slept with Angel," he said and watched her face go from curious to incredulous.

"The one who just murdered people at the palace?" Eden asked, her eyes wide as her hands gripped his tightly.

He nodded.

"That's a lot to take in. How do you feel about it?" she asked. "Are you okay?"

"I honestly don't know," he replied. "I just mentioned it, so you knew my relationship history."

"Oh!" she said before frowning. "Am I expected to give you my whole history as well?"

"But that wasn't . . ." he began before turning red.

"That wasn't your whole relationship history," she said. "You're about ten years older than me. It's to be expected." She shrugged but her cheeks were red as well.

"Did you love her?" she asked, taking the conversation in another direction.

Gideon's eyes slid away as familiar shame washed over him.

"You did," Eden said, taking her hands out of his and clasping them in front of her.

"No! But we gr-grew up together," Gideon started to stutter out, but Eden interjected.

"How did it end?" she asked. "I mean, I know how she ended, but how did your relationship with her end?"

Gideon was silent as there was so much to unpack in the telling of the story. The parts that impacted Lily and Gabe were not his to tell. And truth be told, he was afraid of losing Eden, but he did not want to lie.

Frustrated, he ran a hand through his hair. "It didn't end well."

Seeing that Eden was expecting more, he continued, "Her father chose to die in her place."

Eden gasped and stepped away, looking at him with horror.

He panicked as his hopes of a relationship were fading in front of him. He wanted to rage at the heavens, he was so frustrated. But instead, he decided a strategic retreat was in order.

"I should get my day started," he muttered and moved to the door, but just as his hand touched it, her hand came to rest atop his. Startled, he turned to face her.

"I'm sorry," she said. "It's not every day you find out your boyfriend's ex was a murderer."

He smiled at her use of the word 'boyfriend.' He found it cute and gratifying at the same time. As he leaned closer to kiss her, his conscience tugged at him. "You're agreeing to my mother's plan?" he asked with raised eyebrows.

Eden mock frowned and leaned closer to him as well. "That's a serious concern, but I think I can bear the difficulty."

"You are saying my mother is difficult?" Gideon responded, but there was laughter in his voice which he tried to control. "I'm not laughing."

"Oh, I think you are," Eden replied with a smile, but it was replaced with a frown as she looked away. "We were supposed to talk. Was I too presumptuous?"

"Not at all!" Gideon replied as he clasped her to him. "I'm a hundred percent in. I'm worried that you don't understand what it means to be my girlfriend."

"I think I have an idea," Eden mumbled. "I live here, remember. Plus, I hang out with Lily sometimes."

Gideon tightened his hold on her as he gazed at her face. His heart skipped a beat at her beauty. He wanted desperately to kiss her, but he could not vouch for his control. Plus, he needed to explain to her that if they were married, any male children they had would be in line to the throne, not Amara and Aditya. But it seemed like too weighty a topic for a new relationship. With a sigh, he stepped back.

"It's a lot more pressure being the girlfriend than being the ward," he explained. "Everything will be scrutinized—what you wear, eat, who you talk with. Plus—"

"Gideon, take a breath. I know the risks. I've watched Lily turn herself inside out trying to do the job of island princess."

"But . . ." Gideon did not know how to explain the next concern.

"I also know from Lily that only male heirs can inherit the throne, so there is absolutely no pressure on whoever you marry."

Gideon's reply was a wry smile, but he was a bit shocked that Lily had discussed the matter with Eden. Nonetheless, he was relieved she knew.

"There is a medical procedure . . ."

"We're not there yet, right?" Eden asked. "Can't we take it one day at a time?"

"But if it doesn't work out, we have to go back to plan A and the media will vilify you."

Gideon held his breath, waiting for Eden's response.

"My place in this family was always going to be temporary," Eden began. "I've always needed an exit strategy. But you made me reconsider what it would be like to make this family my forever family. There is no risk-free way to figure that out . . . but if you're willing, then I'm willing to see where this takes us. I choose you."

Gideon gently clasped her hands and raised them to his mouth before placing a kiss on the back of each, his eyes never leaving hers. "I promise I will not let you be hurt," he vowed.

Eden blushed. "Okay, now that we've got that settled, let's discuss Angel. You have to stop carrying the weight of her guilt," she said, her voice surprisingly firm.

At his confused expression, she looked down and then took a breath. "Sometimes, I see you struggle. You can only carry your own guilt. You are not responsible for her becoming a killing machine," she said.

His heart overflowed with gratitude for her earnest conviction. He felt as if a heavy weight had been lifted. The certainty that Eden was the right one for him slid into his heart, into his bones, into the essence that made him himself.

Feeling his own eyes water, he thought, *And that's why I love you.*

At Eden's gasp, he realized he had said the words, not just thought them. He felt embarrassed but pleased as he saw pleasure suffuse her face.

"Eden," he said softly, intently.

As she raised her gaze to his, he leaned in and kissed her. He meant to only give one kiss, but one kiss turned into several, each one deeper than the last. Finally, she put her hand on his chest and pushed.

"We have to meet with other people around," she said.

"We do," he said stupidly, still in a haze from the kisses.

His watch beeped, and the name that popped up cleared the haze.

"My mother," he said to Eden, shaking his head. "This situation has her wound up. It makes her difficult."

Eden nodded sympathetically. She knew all too well.

Gideon continued, "I'm running around, dealing with all this death, with Ya Ya and Brother Adam. And then the islanders' deaths from the ball."

"That's a lot," Eden agreed.

"And then, my mom, who is, by the way, responsible for what happened to Aditya and Amara, decides she needs to treat me like I'm less than twelve."

"Or maybe your mother is afraid I wouldn't know how to behave properly," Eden said, her eyes downcast. His heart turned over as he saw her hands twist together.

Before he could answer, there was a knock on the door. They looked at each other with resignation.

"Two minutes!" Eden called out before looking at Gideon again. "Is there any way you can help Lily?" At Gideon's blank look, Eden rushed to explain. "Lily's aunt is extremely ill, and Lily planned to take a day trip to see her after the funerals here. But Gabe is saying she can't leave?" Eden shook her head. "I'm not sure what is going on. Lily called me hysterically crying, and I could hear the twins wailing in the background."

Gideon realized Eden did not know that the ruling monarch could dictate whether any islander could leave the island. It was a duty that had been delegated to Gabe. Generally, there were royal rules in place for criminals who tried to flee. Gideon could not think of a single instance in which a royal family member had not been allowed to travel.

"I'll look into it," he said.

There was a knock on the door again, this time louder and more demanding. Annoyed, he went to the door and yanked it open.

It was Gabe, whose blood shot eyes, and haggard appearance attested to little sleep. Standing behind him was a frowning Mr. Mann.

"Have you forgotten your obligations?" Gabe snidely asked. "Your father is sick, grandmother is dead, our step-grandfather is dead, islanders are dead. Everyone's dead, but you decide to make out with your American girlfriend." He said Eden's nationality like it was a slur.

Gideon snapped back, "If this is how you talk to your wife, no wonder she wants to leave."

Gabe staggered back as though Gideon had hit him.

"Gideon, Lily doesn't want to leave him!" Eden exclaimed. "She just wants to visit her aunt in Saved America. Why would you say such a thing?"

"Lily's aunt lives in the UK," Gideon replied warily.

"Does she?" Eden responded with a puzzled frown. "Maybe I mixed things up and she has another relative—Oh!"

Gideon could see comprehension dawn as Eden remembered that Asier lived in Saved America.

"Go after him," she dictated, pointing her finger in the direction that Gabe had just gone. "He must be hurting a lot."

Gideon sighed. "You're right. I'll call you tonight?"

At Eden's nod, he moved to hug her goodbye but was stopped by Mr. Mann's discreet cough. The man gave Gideon a hard look. Gideon realized he should have discussed where things stood with Eden's father before now. He really needed to get a grip on things.

"Later," he said to Mr. Mann as he strode quickly away.

GIDEON'S CHANCES TO speak with either his brother or Mr. Mann were limited. On the king's order, the island shut down for a week to mourn the national tragedies that had occurred. Flags remained lowered and schools and workplaces closed. No new fictional series debuted on TV or through the streaming services. The news showed an unrelenting display of grim and grieving faces. Public parks remained open as a way for people to socialize and grieve together. The churches also saw their attendance go up as islanders sought spiritual relief from their collective grief.

For three days and two nights, the country mourned en masse the dead from the palace massacre, the king's mother, and her spouse, Brother Adam. Thousands came through the Plaza of the Dead every hour to bow at the pictures of the deceased on altars laden with flowers. The grieving families greeted as many mourners as they could, ignoring the few who seemed to attend just for the food served as they sat shamelessly at the long tables hastily arranged for the mourners.

"How are you doing?" Eden asked him on day two as she looked up at him while standing by his side.

Gideon gave her a brief nod. If he spoke, he would break down. He had no reserves left. By custom, a family member had to be available for the entire three-day mourning period. He had taken the overnight shift the first night. Gabe had agreed to handle the second night. A night without sleep left Gideon feeling raw, as though his skin had been unkindly scrubbed with an abrasive substance. By the third day, still tired after a night of fractured sleep, Gideon was numb.

Hour upon hour passed as he did nothing but accept condolences, some sincere, some not. He wanted to run back to the hospital and tell his Ya Ya to wake up. He knew she would have a smart comment to make if she could attend her own funeral. He felt an intense longing to see her alive.

The grief of the other families compounded his own, raising the dying embers of guilt to their accustomed roaring flame. Each wail felt like a slashing knife, and he had to struggle not to flinch.

Overcome with the scope of his emotions, Gideon made the decision to step away, but before he could move, he felt hesitant fingers on his back and then a hand pressed more firmly.

"We're almost there," Eden whispered, and he stayed.

Finally, it was all over. The crowd bowed low to the ground three times, and the pictures were placed facedown. In a blur, formalities were observed, until finally they were all back at the palace, in the relative privacy of the family quarters. Staff had put out light dinner fare, but no one was eating.

Gideon sat on the overlarge sofa with his brother, while his mother sat in her favorite gold-and-blue-stripped chair, looking with concern at her ashen-faced husband. The king stood tense, looking at the atrium that had limited light at night. The plants that naturally gravitated toward the sunlight during the day looked like sinister tentacles at night. The only relief from the somber mood was Lily and Eden playing somewhat desultorily with the twins as they energetically played on the floor, happy to see their recently absent parents.

"Be quiet!" the king shouted.

Everyone froze except the twins. While Amara started crying, Aditya repeated the king's instructions, "Be quiet! Be quiet!"

Lily and Eden hurriedly escorted them from the room.

"You should never have married her," the queen said with a snide aside to Gabe as she moved to stand by her husband.

Gideon's mouth tightened as he braced for another round of criticisms, but his brother surprised him.

"If you can't stand my wife or children, we can always move to the UK," he said dispassionately, but his eyes were flashing and resolute.

Gideon looked at his brother in shock. He never would have thought such an idea was in his head. Apparently, the queen felt the same as she gasped, looking back and forth between the king and her oldest son.

"I will not allow it," the king said, his tone quite firm.

"I was not asking for permission," Gabe replied as he stood and stared hard at his father.

"Gabe!" the queen yelled.

"What?" Gabe sniped back. "You got my nanny killed and almost got my daughters killed. But did you apologize even once? Instead, you tried to blame my wife. If you weren't my mother—"

Gideon jumped up before his brother could finish. "Enough! Let's talk when we have calmed down."

Gabe walked out without saying another word. Gideon turned to do the same but noticed his father swaying.

"Father," he said, putting out a hand to help his father.

"I'm calling medical," the queen said as she held on to the king with one hand and with her other hand brought her watch phone to her mouth.

Gideon nodded to his mother but then winced as his father grabbed his still outstretched arm.

"Make sssurre," his father spoke with a slur. "Musst do ex-ex . . ."

"Executions?" Gideon inserted.

His father nodded and then fainted completely.

Two days later, Gideon walked past numerous guards into his father's recovery room. His father had fainted from stress and overwork but was on the mend. He looked over at the door as Gideon entered, his eyebrows raised in question.

"It's done," Gideon said.

"How is it done? Nothing was on the news?"

"I decided against a public spectacle," Gideon said.

The king struggled to sit fully up, but his expression was not pleased. Just then, Gideon's eyes caught the television that was on.

"Look, Father!" he exclaimed as talking heads explained how the remaining Seven members had been executed by being put to permanent sleep via gas.

"That's weak," his father said.

"It's done," Gideon said as he left the room.

A few days later, Gideon stood in front of a microphone facing a sea of reporters. He had spent more time than he would have liked over the last two days being prepped for possible questions. He expected a number of questions on the attack and subsequent executions, so most of the prep time had been spent with the lawyers, security specialists, and Communications wrangling over how much detail should be included in his scripted responses.

The room was packed with domestic and foreign media. They all looked at him with a certain avid hunger that made him want to squirm. But he held still and steady as the Minister of Communications team had coached him and addressed the first question.

"My sister-in-law has briefly left the country to visit a sick relative. My brother went with her. We expect them both back tomorrow."

"Is it true that she can't leave the country without permission?" a British reporter called out.

Gideon ignored that question and called on another reporter.

"What is going on with Eden Edwards? Are you in a relationship with her?"

Gideon had been coached on this question, but he paused before giving the scripted answer. At his pause, the reporters leaned even further forward, hands posed above keyboards or notepads. Their respective camera crews were told to move in for close-ups.

He was not vain, but he knew the clip of his speaking would be replayed multiple times for maximum viewers and ratings. But he only cared about one viewer—Eden. She was watching the press conference from another room with Mr. Mann. His Minister of Communications who stood to the side of the room seemed to sense he was about to go off script and subtly shook her head.

"Yes," he replied, permitting himself a small smile. "I am in a sincere relationship with Ms. Edwards."

The room erupted into pandemonium. "When did you start dating? Was it when she was still a minor? Does the king approve?"

He held up his hand. "This press conference is primarily to address questions on the unprecedented attack on the palace. Any questions related to that?"

11

EDEN, IS LOVE ENOUGH?

I could not stop the smile that had spread across my face at Gideon's words. After the mass funeral, the stress in the family room, my helping Lily get the twins to bed, and the king being rushed to the infirmary, our time together had been rather limited. His words were reassuring. As a double-plus, only Mr. Mann was with me in the conference room, so I did not have to worry about others watching my expression.

Did you see? Gideon texted me immediately afterward.

Yes, I saw you go off script, I texted back, thought about it, and then added a heart emoji.

Let's carve out time to talk tomorrow?

Okay, I replied, wishing we could talk sooner.

Unfortunately, the press conference earlier in the day resulted in my phone pinging non-stop from college classmates and others who I didn't know but suspected were press. In addition, folks from the Minister of Communications Office presented me with statement options but advised me to give none just yet. I was somewhat surprised not to be summoned by the queen.

After a long day of "no comments," I had dragged my tired form to my suite, taken the second-shortest shower in history, and then fallen onto the bed in an exhausted heap. And I stayed wide awake.

My mind was clouded with worries and uncertainty. *What was happening with the king? Would Lily get to see Asier? Would she and Gabe break up? Was that even possible for a member of the royal family? Would Gideon want to marry me? Did I want to marry him?* I had always assumed my feelings for him were a bit of a fantasy. *So, what does one do with a fantasy coming to life?* And on this thought, I fell into an uneasy sleep where I dreamed an uneasy dream.

In my dream, I stood side by side with Gideon, holding hands. Stringed music played in the background, and island flowers released a lovely fragrance. In the way of dreams, I knew there were many people around and that it was night. We happily smiled at each other. Gideon wore a black suit, white shirt, and no tie. I wore a flowing ivory silk and lace dress. I turned, expecting to see a minister, but instead, there was another bride, an island bride. And Gideon was standing beside her. Confused, I turned back to the Gideon I was holding hands with and saw only a standing, grinning skeleton. Gasping, I woke up. That's the only reason I heard my watch phone buzz on the nightstand.

It was Gideon. He had texted, *Are you still up? I'm at the door.*

I hurriedly texted back, *One sec.*

When I opened the door, no one was there. I had almost closed the door to go text him, when I saw him. He sat on the floor, his head leaning against the wall, fast asleep. I could see the stress of the day in the dark circles under his eyes, the deeper grooves in his face, and the general cloud of weariness that had shrouded him since the attack.

I sat next to him, thinking we would talk when he awakened. The next thing I knew, I was being shaken awake.

"What?" I mumbled, burrowing my head more firmly into what I thought was my pillow, but something did not feel right.

Sleepily opening my eyes, I saw Gideon's still-tired-but-amused gaze on my face and realized I had been sleeping with my head on his shoulder cushioned by a pillow. Abruptly, I sat up and then screamed as I saw Mrs. Wright's smug face looming over me.

She winced at my scream and stood up. "Your behavior is most inappropriate."

"You don't scream when you wake up to find someone looming over you?" I replied, my tone sharper than advisable as I tried to gather my wits.

"Mrs. Wright, please give us ten minutes," Gideon interjected in his most charming voice as he stood.

"I'll be right around the corner," she warned as she stiffly walked off.

I looked up at Gideon and groaned as I felt a crick in my neck.

Gideon held out a hand and helped me stand. "What's wrong?" he asked as he saw a frown flit across my face.

"This pillow," I replied as I held it up with the hand that was not holding his. "I could have sworn I did not have a pillow when I opened the door last night."

"You did not," he replied with a slow smile that made me want to lean closer. "You were drooling on me in your sleep, so I went to get your pillow."

"I don't drool!" I exclaimed.

"Shhh!" Gideon said, holding a finger to his mouth. "You want to bring Mrs. Wright back?"

My expression gave him my answer, and he laughed softly while pulling me closer.

"Are you still fine with us going off plan?" he whispered.

I nodded, surprised he would even ask with the way things had been going between us.

He pulled back, only to lean in for a kiss. I closed my eyes in anticipation but then heard steps clicking rapidly towards us.

"It's been ten minutes," Mrs. Wright's voice came from behind me. It could not have been more than five minutes.

With a sign of resignation, Gideon kissed me on the forehead and departed, leaving me alone with Mrs. Wright. I turned and gave her a tight smile.

"The queen is asking for you," she said brightly. Her predatory smile let me know that the queen would not be in a good mood.

"I'll get dressed . . ." I started to say.

"No, Ms. Edwards. She said to come immediately."

Then why did you give me those minutes with Gideon? I thought to myself. I hated the thought of parading through the palace halls in pajamas and enduring the sideways glances that were sure to follow. The queen would surely not be amused.

"I guess I'll have to be done quickly, then," I said as I escaped to my suite.

Fifteen minutes later, I was more presentable and hurried after an annoyed Mrs. Wright. Instead of leading me to the queen's office as I expected, she led me to the king and queen's private royal suite. Their rooms were much larger than mine and were more of a full-scale apartment, done up in blue, gold, and ivory colors.

Mrs. Wright led me to their private sitting room. As I entered, the queen got up from the sofa and walked over to me, giving me her own version of the tight smile.

Smack! The sound split the air as a hard palm smacked against my cheek.

I stumbled a few steps to the side, cradling my injured cheek with one hand while I held the other hand out as if to warn the queen away.

"You can go now, Mrs. Wright," the queen said.

The queen slapped me and wanted a witness? I straightened my posture and looked over at the queen, my hands balled into tight fists to remind myself not to lash out. Wetness threatened to spill from my eyes as anger, fear, and confusion warred within me. The queen had never struck me.

"You are a disgrace," she said, venom and scorn lacing her voice as she started to circle me. "To think I took you in and gave you a home, and this is how you repay me?"

"Your Highness, I have no idea—" I began, but she moved to slap me again. Without consciously thinking, I blocked her by grabbing her raised arm by the wrist and then held her other wrist when she raised her other arm. Looking at our positions and remembering that she was the queen, I released her and jumped back as though scalded.

The queen's body went slack, and she fell to the floor.

I rushed to her prone figure, frantically asking if she was all right, but she was nonresponsive. With one hand on her shoulder, I used my other shaky hand to press the house emergency line on my watch phone.

"Confirm location?" requested a tinny mechanical voice.

"R—MS," I stumbled through the initials for the Ruling Monarch Suite.

Within a couple of minutes, the double doors to the suite flew open and a bunch of royal guards swarmed in with weapons drawn.

"Move away from the queen!"

I stared at them with my mouth open, not moving even when the command was repeated in both English and Sorean. It was only when the guns rose that I understood my horrific predicament.

Danger! My brain screeched, and I scrambled back, only to find myself grabbed and flung face down on the ground as my wrists were handcuffed. The female guard sitting astride my back grabbed a fistful of hair and slammed my head to the ground.

"I called—" I started to say, but then my head was slammed down again. I felt the pain in my jaw and my mouth as I tasted blood.

My head was facing the queen, and I dizzily watched as she slowly sat up, a confused expression on her face.

"Eden, why did you attack me? After all we've done for you?" she asked as two guards helped her stand.

Chills went through me at her words. As I stared up at her through narrowed eyes, I could see a sly look cross her face, but I doubted if anyone else would. She was completely believable.

"Yes, I saw it all," a shocked voice said. It was Mrs. Wright. "Eden shoved our queen."

I thought she had left. I closed my eyes to the nightmare unfolding before me.

"What's going on here?" I heard Gideon query.

I tried to move my head to see him, but the guard straddling me only tightened her hold. Afraid of another head slam, I kept still.

Gideon came to stand next to his mother, who collapsed into his arms crying. He looked at me with no expression, as though I were nothing, and turned away with his mother.

I started to shake as my tears continued to fall.

"They always start crying after the fact," a disgusted voice said.

"Let's get her processed," someone else said as the female guard got off my back.

Two male guards yanked me up, their monstrous-sized hands squeezing my arms painfully. As they dragged me toward the double doors, I was frantic at the thought of Gideon misunderstanding. I turned my head back, ruthlessly ignoring the thousand shards of hurt that caressed my neck.

"Gideon, please help me," I begged.

He did not respond, his cold gaze spearing me with utter rejection. His arms continued to hold his mother.

I was dragged out and taken through another door, a side one I had never noticed. Narrow, high stone walls greeted us. There was only enough room for three to walk abreast, me and two guards. Guards were to the front and back of us. After long minutes, we reached another door with a staircase.

"Don't try anything," the guard on my left warned.

I nodded, unable to speak through the intense pain on the side of my face.

We went down the stairs and into another long hallway before coming out into the security section. Staff stopped and stared. Hot, virulent shame rushed through me, cruelly spiking my blooming headache to an almost unbearable level. I swayed from the onslaught before silently praying, *Lord, help me.*

"What is happening?" a hard voice demanded. It was Mr. Mann.

"Bad business, and not yours," came the harsh reply. "She's wanted for royal crimes."

Mr. Mann politely bowed and stepped out of the way. I bit my lip to keep from crying out, "Father, save me." I would only doom him too.

But then he said, "Act the truth you know."

The guards looked at each other and shrugged before pulling me forward.

I looked back, and Mr. Mann nodded once he saw I understood.

When I was about eight or nine, I went with my parents to a

church picnic. They had stations set up for the kids to play games. I remembered tripping over my own feet during a sack race. Afterward, Eliza, Mary, and I ran around playing tag, which Mary won as she was the fastest that day. Exhausted from tag, we headed over to the food table, snatching fruit-juice-sweetened dessert when the adults were not looking and stuffing our faces until our cheeks bulged. The parents were too busy chatting to pay us attention. After playing some more, we finally dropped into an exhausted heap onto the grass.

The sense of freedom was satisfying, and my younger self thought it was the most perfect day ever. Or at least it was until Cassie, Eliza's little sister, came over.

"Eliza, why can't I play with you," she whined.

"Go away," Eliza said, refusing to even open her eyes to look at Cassie.

Usually, Cassie would start whining more and then Eliza would say something back and then their parents would descend, and Eliza would have to go anyway. But that is not what happened here. In a plot twist, Cassie pointed an accusing finger at Eliza, forgetting that she held an ice cream cone in her other hand and tipped it too far. A perfectly scooped ice cream ball plopped onto my shirt. Startled, I jumped up, and the ice cream fell to the ground.

"Eden stole my ice cream," Cassie cried, still pointing her finger but now at me.

"What a horrible example you're setting, stealing a little girl's ice cream," Cassie and Eliza's mother hissed at me as she picked up a hiccupping and crying Cassie.

By that time, Mary's parents and my own had also come over. I flushed as I felt all eyes on me, and I felt shame at what they must have thought.

"I . . . didn't." It was all I could stammer out before I was saved by Eliza.

"Cassie, stop lying," she retorted. "You know you dropped it." Of course, this simple statement of truth started another round of high-pitched wailing from Cassie.

My father came over and kneeled slightly so he could look me in the face. "Is what Eliza said true?"

I nodded.

"Then stop acting like you did something wrong," my father gently chastised.

I looked at my feet, feeling more confused than ever.

"Act the truth you know," he said a bit impatiently.

I nodded again, but by then, Eliza's mom was scolding Cassie for lying and everyone else moved away.

Today, unlike back then, I understood my father's words. I stood and walked straighter, gazing directly ahead. Unfortunately, my bravado was short-lived. The guard on my right deliberately tripped me, and I stumbled but avoided a full-face plant. As I straightened up, another guard shoved me from behind.

"Hey," a voice shouted.

The guard on the left cursed as Luke and James ran up. I frowned as I braced for their disappointment. James's unusually severe expression made my stomach churn.

He looked at the guards and said, "You all are relieved from duty, immediately."

"But . . ."

James stiffened. "That was a direct order."

"But the queen's—" another guard tried this time.

"You gave an oath to behave honorably. You have behaved dishonorably. Give way."

As the guards slinked away, Luke and James carefully took my arms and guided me to a side room in the security section. Luke took off my restraints and indicated that I should sit on the lone chair, the one piece of furniture in an otherwise drab, windowless room. I sat gingerly, expecting them to question me, but they left quickly.

Sitting still, I could feel the pain from being grabbed and slammed. My neck felt sore, my head ached, and my arms hurt. I pulled down one section of my shirt to look at my arm. Angry red bruises circled all the way around my upper arm, the sight of which broke the dam of surrealness.

Shaking uncontrollably, I put my head in my hands and sobbed. How did I lose everything so quickly? Every loss began to run together: the loss of my original home, my school, my friends—Eliza, Mary, Kaitlyn, Bethany, and more painful losses that had to be locked in a corner attic in my mind. I only peeked into it every once in a while when memories demanded a visit.

Now, though, the attic was a hoarder's dream, full to bursting as it held the loss of my mother, the loss of whatever connection I had with Dr. Brown, my ability to be recognized as my father's daughter, the new family I thought I had found, and Gideon.

The attic door shuddered before splintering open, grief gushing out in tsunami-like waves until I just curled into a ball on the cold floor, shivering and spent.

But I could not deny that a small kernel of anger had taken root in my soul, and as I fell into an exhausted sleep, my dreams were troubled. They were but wisps of images and impressions, but my heart pounded in fear of some unnamed danger.

I felt hands shaking me and opened my mouth to scream, but instead I gasped as I came awake and saw Gideon sitting beside me on the floor, his hand and gaze focused on a reddish purple bruise on my arm.

"What are you doing?" I asked, my voice hoarse.

He removed his hand and started to speak, closed his mouth, and then tried again. "Waiting for you to wake up so I could beg forgiveness," he said before his gaze dropped to my arm again. "Your bruises look aw—ful." His voice trembled slightly but he continued. "My mother's been taken to get treatment."

I pushed myself to a sitting position, my head swimming with the effort. But I kept my face blank so Gideon could not see.

"There was something off about her medication which caused her to act differently," he further explained.

Or more like herself, I thought.

"I'm sorry about the way I acted earlier," he said as he reached for me, his eyes begging me to understand.

I leaned away. "I understand." I didn't.

A pained look crossed his face.

"I'm sorry," he reiterated.

"Am I free to go?" I asked, but before he could respond, Luke and James came in. Luke frowned, but James smiled as he handed me a bottle of juice and a warm face cloth. I hurriedly wiped my face and took fortifying sips of the juice as Gideon stood and conversed with the guards. His gaze, however, remained on me. Uncomfortable with sitting on the floor while three men stood around me, I stood, using the chair as leverage, and tuned into the conversation.

"Sir, we were able to delete all copies on the video feed on palace servers," Luke was saying.

Gideon averted his gaze from me. "Thanks, but give me a few more minutes with Eden."

The guards promptly left.

"Video?" I asked, wondering if the security cameras caught my perp walk of shame.

Gideon nodded but looked down at his shoes, his hands in his pants pockets. An uncomfortable prickling scratched my neck.

"What video?" I asked again.

Gideon was silent, but then he looked at me, his whole posture one of defeat. The prickling grew stronger.

"My mother had requested a camera in her suite to catch a house-keeping staff member whom she suspected of theft."

Thinking quickly, I asked, "Did the camera catch—"

Gideon nodded before I finished.

No, it could not be, I thought to myself, but I had to confirm. The whole incident had been recorded. Gideon must have believed his mother before he watched the video.

"Did you see the video before you—"

Again, Gideon nodded before I could finish. And just like that, any tiny flare of hope was extinguished, replaced by a sense of betrayal so deep every part of me felt ill. Nauseous, I took a shaky step back and slipped, but before I could fall, Gideon caught me and hauled me against him, his arms tight against me.

"The floor is wet with your tears," he despaired, his hands rubbing my back, and for a moment, I wanted to accept the meager comfort of his embrace. Instead, I took a deep breath, pushed his arms away, and stepped back. I could not pretend.

"Eden . . ." he implored as he reached for me again, grabbing my listless hand.

"Why?" I asked, taking my hand back.

"I . . . she's my mom . . . and the queen," he stammered out, seemingly surprised by my question. "I could not correct her in front of others."

The worst part of it all was that I did understand. It had been drilled into me that the image of the crown must be protected at all costs. Even if innocent people suffered, it was for the greater good—the stability and welfare of the island. I had never taken that lesson to heart, secretly rebelling at the idea that evil could be allowed if one was royal enough.

"Do you realize what you've done?" I whispered. "You allowed me to be utterly humiliated and disgraced, for an absolute lie. And you thought so little of me that you thought we could continue?"

"That's not it . . ." He reached out again.

I shook my head and held my hands up.

His hands dropped, but his eyes kept pleading.

I closed my eyes. "I guess it's back to the original plan," I said, my voice wobbly.

"We can try . . ." he began.

I shook my head and shuffled away, my arms wrapped tightly around my middle. I had only taken a few steps when he hugged me from behind.

"We can't let it end like this," he said unsteadily as his breath caressed my cheek.

God, help me! I thought to myself.

"When *should* it end?" I asked without turning around. "The next time I become inconvenient?" I could not keep the bite out of my voice.

"What else could I have done?" he asked, his arms tightening around me.

"Defended me. Chosen *me*," I snapped back.

But he could never choose me. I would always be dead last, after the king, queen, brother, and kingdom. And just like that, reality kicked the anger out, bringing an oversized order of sadness in its place.

THE NEXT DAY, I woke up disoriented. I reached for my watch phone and saw that it was already midday. No one had come knocking on my door. I wondered if Mrs. Wright had been fired for yesterday. I could not prevent a small feeling of satisfaction at the thought as I stretched and yawned myself awake.

Having another thought, I reached for my watch phone again, but it had suddenly become disconnected from the web. After fiddling with it for unproductive minutes, I reached for my regular phone, only to see that the web was disconnected on it as well. I had wanted to see if I had a text from Gideon, even though I knew I should not have even looked. I also knew I would check in a few moments, when the electronic glitch was fixed.

Standing to take a shower on unsteady legs, I first grabbed a bar from my in-room stash and some water. Feeling more human, I shuffled to the washroom, grateful I had another day or so before I had to go back to class. A few intense weeks of studying and exams, and then it would be time for another break.

A knock finally came just as I finished pulling my favorite Island University sweatshirt over my head. Mr. Mann looked at me with something like relief.

"You look okay," he said, but I could tell it was a question.

Not sure how to answer, I shrugged and moved back to let him in.

"Are you okay?" he asked directly, his gaze searching.

"I've been a bit foolish," I admitted, not meeting his gaze. "I need to focus on my future away from the palace, away from . . . everything."

It was his turn to look confused. "I was talking about today's news," he said.

"The web was out," I said, moving toward my bedroom. "Let me check it now."

"Wait!" he said. "Leave it be for now. Don't check anything, not even the TV."

"What is going on?" I asked, turning to look at him, surprised at his vehemence.

"I can't tell you," he said with a grimace. "But I know someone who can. You'll know by the end of today."

And with those words, he left.

Feeling a little bit like Eve in the Garden of Eden, I sat on the sofa and leaned my head back, my mind and body still weary from yesterday's revelations.

In the fractured dream that followed, I stood barefoot on vibrant green grass, the feeling of crushed blades beneath my feet reassuring me that I stood on solid ground. I was in an orchard filled with young to old trees, some slender as a reed and others so wide you could carve a small home inside of them. Fruit in every imaginable color—red, orange, yellow, light green, black—hung in various shapes from the trees, their ripe scents flooding my nose and teasing my tongue, which salivated in anticipation of tasting rich sweetness.

But there was an anomaly, a mid-sized tree with phones instead of fruit. Electricity zapped up and down the tree, giving off sparks, but the phones were glitchy.

"Just one touch, and you'll know," a reptilian voice said.

I wanted to turn my head to see who—or what—spoke, but my head was in a vise, and I could only look straight at the tree. Suddenly, I was so thirsty for knowledge.

Reaching out my hand, I was startled to see that my hand was not human but robotic, the tips sharp metal. Looking down, I realized I was no longer human, and I howled in despair, falling to knees that crunched when I fell.

A soft knock on the door brought me back to myself. I am not ashamed to admit I did a quick reassuring body scan before I got up to open the door.

12

GIDEON, READY OR NOT

"*Her* web access is cut?" Gideon asked, confirming that his order had been followed.

Gideon looked at the Minister of Communications, who gave him a tightlipped smile and miniscule bow. Gideon resisted the urge to throw something. He needed to make things right with Eden. She had held up a mirror for him, and he despised what he saw. He thought he was stronger morally after Angel, but he had caved to his mother's lies without thought. Eden was right, he had treated her abominably. He had to fix this situation. He needed to show her that the next time he would choose her. And hope that she would come back to him. But his family was also choosing this moment to need him. How many masters could one person serve?

Frustrated, he pinged his assistant and asked for multiple bouquets of island flowers to be delivered to Eden as soon as humanly possible.

Gideon returned his attention to the minister, whose face was completely neutral. Sometimes Gideon wondered if she thought they worked for her, as opposed to the other way around. Today, however, he did not wonder. He just needed her to thread a mystical spindle and spin gold out of the mess that was the royal family.

Rubbing his hand through his already tousled hair, Gideon said, "Okay, play it again please."

The screen showed Gideon's brother and sister-in-law walking quickly through the airport surrounded by security. Gabe was holding a child, who Gideon now recognized as Asier. Word of their presence on a commercial flight had gotten out, so there was a sizable media presence surrounding them. Gideon knew his brother had made it back to the palace with Lily and Asier, but he cringed inside as he saw how easily things could have turned if the media hounds circling his brother with hungry eyes had known Asier's status. More than one famous person had died in the frenzy of a media attack.

"They actually put out a statement?" Gideon asked rhetorically since he held the statement in his hand.

"Right after they arrived at the palace, with no word to any member of the royal family or the Communications team." It was clear to Gideon that the minister viewed not telling the Communications team as the most significant error.

With a sigh, he looked around the minister's office, noting the gold and orange color scheme, a suitable backdrop for the minister who looked like a modern-day Queen Elizabeth I as she sat in a burnt orange pantsuit.

Sitting in the Communications team's main conference room at a round table with other Communications staff, Gideon felt at a distinct disadvantage. Normally, the minister would come to the royals' offices, but he'd felt like stretching his legs, so he'd come to her. Now he felt like a fly caught in a web of disguised barbs. Futilely, he looked at the statement again.

I, Gabriel Li, son of King Edward and Queen Jasmine, and Crown Prince of Seahorse Island, hereby make my abject apologies to my family, including my son Asier, and the citizens of Seahorse Island.

The letter went on in some detail about how they had deceived everyone by declaring their son dead. He had been born with a Tiger claw defect and was sent to live with an adoptive family in Untouchable City. The adoptive parents had passed away, so they were taking their son back.

"A terrible miscalculation," the minister said as she looked at something on her electronic notepad.

Gideon looked sharply across the table at her, his face a mask of displeasure at her criticism.

She held up a hand. "My apologies. I should not have criticized Prince Gabriel. But it still stands that the public will never accept his child."

"Can't you make it so that they will?" Gideon asked.

She shook her head. "For all its trappings of modern life, the island is still extremely superstitious."

"I disagree," Gideon replied, and he walked around the table so that he stood next to her. "We could weather this storm." He strongly felt that bringing his nephew home was the right thing to do. He had never agreed with the decision to send him away.

The minister shook her head as she stood, leaning toward him with her notepad pushed in his direction so he could see as well. "Look at these numbers."

Gideon frowned and then winced. A solid seventy-five percent of those polled thought Prince Gabriel Li and his wife, Princess Lily Li, were bringing bad luck to the island by bringing Asier home. Just under fifteen percent thought it suspicious that both of Asier's adoptive parents died. Gideon frowned; he had not asked Gabriel how they died.

"How many people were polled?" he asked as he searched the screen for that information.

"Five thousand from each sector," she replied.

"He's a child," Gideon said incredulously. "Besides, you can't possibly have polled that many people so quickly."

The minister shook her head. "It's a popular poll, with many of the public wanting to weigh in. It's still up."

"Shut it down," Gideon ordered.

The minister nodded but then pressed her lips together. "Think of all the royal families whom we know. None have any known or visible diseases or defects."

"But it's different now," Gideon interjected impatiently. "There's all the testing to make sure everything's genetically fine."

"Then what happened with Asier?"

"That's not what I meant," Gideon said, his fingers shoving his hair back in exasperation.

"Sir, it may not be what you meant, but that is exactly how island citizens think," she stated.

Gideon cursed, his hands gripping the back of the chair in front of him. "How can we spin this?"

"I will have to be removed from the line of succession," Gabriel said as he came into the room.

"Are you crazy?" Gideon yelled at his brother.

"Not anymore," his brother replied, standing next to Gideon, who didn't like the resolve he saw on his brother's face.

"Look, you did the right thing with Asier," Gideon began, placing a hand briefly on his brother's shoulder. "I can't wait to officially meet my nephew. But you cannot stop being the crown prince."

Gabe shook his head. "If I have to choose between Asier and the crown, Asier comes out the winner."

"The public will come around," Gideon scoffed. "Besides, communal leaders would have to approve your removal."

"Leave us," Gabe told the Communications team. The staff all hastily left except the minister.

She asked, "Do I need to stay?"

"Don't worry," Gabe cajoled. "You can expect no more blindsides. We'll keep you in the loop." He gave her a brilliant smile as he held the door open for her. She gave a small dip of her head as she left, but her reluctance was clear.

"I'm surprised you felt the need to explain," Gideon said after the minister left. "You normally just say no when she asks that question."

"As the crown prince, I could get away with a lot," his brother said with a shrug. "But in this case, I'm not sure what my family's status will be after I'm no longer royal. I'm trying to not burn bridges on my way out."

A rare look of vulnerability on his brother's face unmoored Gideon even more. His mother had become someone he no longer recognized, his father was always grim, he had betrayed whatever was building between him and Eden, and now his brother was talking about being thrown out of the line of succession. Anger, grief, and fear wove a three-stranded rope within him and lassoed a fissured heart.

He grabbed his brother by the shoulders and shook him hard. "Stop it! This situation is utter madness. You can't be thrown out of the family for doing the right thing!"

His brother quickly and firmly pushed Gideon's arms away. "Grow up!" he commanded roughly, but Gideon noticed the catch in his brother's voice and the suspiciously shiny eyes.

Gideon cursed. "Father has already set things in motion?"

Gabriel nodded. "The vote happens within a week." He looked away from Gideon before continuing. "The Communications team is working on tomorrow morning's statement as well as the statement that goes out to each sector head."

Gideon stared at his brother as the magnitude of what was happening became apparent to him. He, Gideon, would become the de facto crown prince and outrank his brother. His nephew would be cut out of the line of succession.

"Why?" he finally asked as he started to pace the room.

His brother shrugged. "Royalty equals perfection. You know that as well as I do."

"None of us are perfect!" Gideon snapped.

"You would know!" his brother retorted.

"Really?" Gideon asked in disbelief.

His brother shook his head. "You're right; not the time. I meant that to the public there needs to at least be an appearance of stability and infallibility."

"And the closer one is to the throne, the stronger that appearance needs to be," Gideon concluded, thinking uncomfortably about his conversation about the queen with Eden, even though the queen was not in the line of succession.

"Exactly," Gabriel agreed. "There's something additional you should remember."

At Gideon's questioning look, Gabe continued, "If the crown prince is removed from the line of succession before death, then that is one of the rare instances in which the three most senior sector heads are automatically appointed as economic advisors for a year."

"I vaguely remember that clause, but I thought it would never happen." Gideon shook his head. "Surely they don't have veto power?"

"No," Gideon assured him. "But they do get access to data they don't have now."

"The three most senior sector heads include . . ." Gideon thought aloud as he rapidly went through names in his head.

"Segenam's dad!" the brothers exclaimed simultaneously. By now Gideon stood on the other side of the conference room table so the brothers wore mirrored expressions of horror.

"But I thought he was going to be replaced by Saduj?" Gideon asked.

"Not yet," his brother said. "Not that he would be better."

"What's your plan now?" Gideon asked.

"Well, I try to figure out some way I can be of service to the family and the island, or we start over in another country. You'll need to get married to Eden."

Gideon forcefully smacked his hands down on the table between them. "That's it? That's your plan? You were born to lead this country, and because of one opinion poll you run away with your tail tucked between your legs? I thought more of you," Gideon said, his disgust evident.

"Gideon . . . " Gabe began.

"Think like a politician and not a father or son," Gideon insisted. "Francisco was caught throwing a raucous birthday party for his mistress while his country's front-line soldiers were dying left and right in battle, and his country reelected him as prime minister. Silvia was caught—"

His brother held up his hand. "I got it. What did you have in mind?"

Gideon grinned and sat down, motioning for his brother to do the same. Gabriel sat; his expression wary.

Gideon started to speak, but his brother held up his hand. "Is there a bomb underneath here?" Gabe asked. "Oh look, it will go off if I move."

Shaking his head at his brother's absurdly poor acting skills, Gideon said nothing but was shocked seconds later when the door opened to a gasping Communications Minister. "Sir, the bomb squad is on its way."

The brothers looked at each other with dismay. After they had straightened out a visibly chastened minister, they walked into the west garden. They could have stayed in the conference room with a sound jammer to avoid being overheard, but they both preferred the garden.

They walked without speaking for some minutes, letting their raging hearts be lulled into relative stillness by the wildness of nature constrained within rigidly maintained patterns of plants and flowers, the setting sun acting as a thermostat to turn down their emotions.

No amount of nature, though, could settle Gideon's uneasiness about Eden. Last night, he had gone to her room and heard the sound of her crying through the door, faint but unerring. He had placed his hands against the door, leaning into it, frustration making him want to pound it. How do you explain that your father and mother, as your king and queen, come first in everything, with any significant others a distant second or third?

In the quiet of the garden, Gideon's heart had no distraction from its longing for Eden, and he realized with a start that she was probably still in her room, wondering what was going on. He looked at his watch again.

"Do you have plans?" Gabe asked.

"What?" Gideon asked, distracted by thoughts of Eden.

"You keep checking the time on your watch phone."

Gideon nodded and thrust his hands into his pants' pockets.

"Everything okay with Eden?" his brother asked.

"No," Gideon replied.

"What happened?" Gabriel asked.

"Mom was being her new normal," he concluded as he lightly kicked at a stray pebble.

"How bad?" Gabe asked.

"Bad. The guards detained Eden."

"What! Tell me everything," his brother commanded as he came to a stop, looking every inch the crown prince.

Even though Gideon was a hair shorter than his brother he was slightly bigger in build, yet all of a sudden, he felt smaller. His brother had sacrificed everything for his family. He, on the other hand, had abandoned and let Eden be publicly humiliated and left her sitting in her room all day in the dark, afraid of the panic she would feel over his brother's situation and the inevitable media questions about their own relationship that would follow.

"I need to talk to Eden now," he said, filled with a sudden urgency. "Let's meet later."

"She's not here," he heard a voice say before Lily came into view. "I took Asier to meet her, but then Mr. Mann came and said she had an overseas engagement in England."

Stunned, Gideon tried to phone Eden, but the call went straight to voicemail. He then called Mr. Mann, pacing the garden as he did so, completely forgetting his brother and sister-in-law.

"Sir?" came Mr. Mann's carefully neutral voice.

"Why is Eden on the way to England?" Gideon's voice was not neutral, more like the hissed sound of an angry snake.

"Was there something for her to do on the island?" Mr. Mann asked. "Her status is unclear at the moment."

Gideon felt the dig and knew he deserved it but was angry neverthe-less. "She belongs at my side," he asserted.

Mr. Mann made a non-committal sound that nonetheless conveyed his skepticism.

Pressing his fingers into his forehead, Gideon took a breath for patience. Before he could speak, however, Mr. Mann did.

"Eden needs time to consider her own thoughts and goals. Her engagements will require her to be in England for the next month and a half. It has been cleared with the king, her school, and Communi-cations."

Recognizing the frost in the man's voice, Gideon treaded lightly. "When can I talk with her?"

"When she chooses to speak with you."

When the call ended, Gabe and Lily had left and the sky was now completely dark, lit up by stars and decoratively strung lights. Sitting on a bench, Gideon placed his head in his hand. He prayed for a path forward on all fronts.

When he sat back up, he realized with some surprise that his hands were damp from tears that had leaked through. He had not been aware of his own tears. Feeling calmer and more peaceful, though, he stared at the stars and strategized.

The next day, he got up and made sure Eden's web access had been restored before typing a text to her.

I'm sorry for everything. Praying that your engagements are fruitful. Be safe and well. His hand hovered over the screen because the message felt incomplete. He needed to be braver and truthful. *P.S. I love you.*

He stared at the screen for a full minute before he realized that with the time difference, she would be sleeping, and even without the time difference, she probably was not sitting around waiting for his text.

Putting the next phase of his plan in motion, he then sent out an all-staff email and copied his family, indicating that no communication—official or otherwise—should be released from the palace that day. He had barely buttoned his suit jacket before his father barged into his suite.

"Have I died?" the king yelled. "Who gave you the authority to stop communication?"

"I did," Gideon said with a final adjustment to his tie, not even looking at his father.

"You've been overruled," his father said as he stormed back to the door.

"I never took you for a coward," Gideon said.

His father stalked back and grabbed him by the collar. "What did you say to me?" he asked, his voice a low, menacing growl.

"Asier was born with a claw face and got sent away. Gabe acknowledges his son and is disinherited. The queen, my mother and your wife, is in a facility because she has lost her mind. The only one left is me, your son who almost killed his brother, the one who drank too much."

His father's face got redder with each word Gideon spoke, but Gideon pressed on.

"Are you the king?" he asked doubtfully. "Or does the media run this island?"

His father released him as though Gideon had struck him.

Contrition squeezing his heart, Gideon reached out. "Father . . ." he began.

But his father walked away.

Gideon closed his eyes, took a deep breath, and walked to his office suite, determined to save his family. His assistant, Plath was waiting for him.

"Sir, Communications has not stopped calling since your email this morning. Your brother also called—"

Gideon held up a hand to stop the flow. "We have other calls to make today."

"We do?" His assistant blinked before looking at his notepad. "I don't see anything listed—"

"There's been a change of plans," Gideon said a bit impatiently.

"Of course," his assistant said with a tight smile.

"I need to call all the sector heads today, one by one."

Gideon pretended not to hear his assistant's under-the-breath murmurings.

A quick glance at the day's headlines revealed that all the sector heads had given comments to the media, similarly expressing dismay and shock at Prince Gabriel's duplicity. With resolve, Gideon got to work.

He started with the Chief of Staff for Sector 13's head. She was often in classes with him and Gabe at school. He was not sure how she obtained her current position as her penchant for straightforward speech made diplomacy difficult for her.

"Prince Gideon," she greeted him simply, no surprise in her voice as her image appeared on the video screen in his office.

Taken off guard for a moment, Gideon leaned back as he asked, "You don't seem surprised to hear from me."

She gave a minuscule shrug. "It's just a matter of deduction, with your current situation."

"Ah, you learned diplomacy," he replied with a smile.

"Well, I could hardly say that your brother's about to be voted out, your mother has medical issues, and your father has checked out."

Gideon felt gut-punched and sat up straight. "Where did you hear such lies?"

"*Glitter Tattle*, a staffer had it on," she replied with a frown. "There was no intent to offend, Prince Gideon."

Gideon nodded and breathed his temper down. "We may need some understanding from the sector heads."

"I believe my sector head will be understanding. He especially supports the royal family's commitment to the new community park that will serve not only Sector 13 but several connecting sectors."

Gideon frowned. "I don't recall—"

But she continued as though he had not spoken. "These sector heads have not overlooked the fact that, until now, their communities were woefully underserved on public amenities, so we sincerely thank the royal family for its support."

Wiser now, Gideon understood what she was getting at. "The royal family is always happy to support all islanders."

With smiles on both sides, the call ended soon thereafter.

At midafternoon, Gabe walked into his office. "Is there any money left in the treasury?"

Gideon held up a hand as he made a note for his next call. When he finished, he noted the recent stress lines on his brother's face.

"It's worth it," he said. "I think I have eleven yeas, two maybes."

His brother nodded approvingly. "That's a majority, but we don't want a divided vote."

Gideon shook his head. "We'll never get Segenam's dad's vote and the two other sector heads who would be on the advisory council."

"We could try to get the king to remove them from office," Gabe said more as a question.

"They have to be removed by their sectors except for blatant incompetence."

The brothers looked at each other before regretfully giving up on that idea.

"We have to give them a way to save face," Gabe acknowledged as he sat back, bringing his fingertips together.

"The palace has withdrawn the motion," the king said without preamble as he walked in.

"But the three most senior sector heads can revive it," Gideon said.

"Segenam's dad doesn't have the support of the other two," his father said. "Your work today paid off."

Gideon's and Gabe's exclamations of relief were cut short by their father's raised hand as he walked farther into the office. Gideon frowned as he noticed a slight hitch in his father's normally smooth gait and the weariness etched on his face as he pulled Gabe and then Gideon into a group hug. Gideon had forgotten the soul-deep comfort of such hugs; it had been so long. The hug was prolonged as relief and gratification surged through all three men.

When the king released them, his eyes were wet with tears. "I am beyond blessed to have sons with wisdom," he said, patting both their arms.

"We were taught well," Gabe quipped, and they laughed.

The king motioned for all of them to sit. Gideon and Gabe sat at the conference table, but the king pulled his chair up behind them, so they turned their chairs around.

The king put his head in his hand, alarming the brothers who looked at each other with unspoken questions.

Finally, the king looked up just as Plath entered with a tea tray.

"Leave us!" the king commanded, his booming voice at odds with his previous demeanor.

The tea tray shook, but the assistant was able to withdraw quickly without spilling anything. Gideon felt a moment of relief as his attention returned to his father.

"Gabe, you will need to act as prince regent," the king said.

"Wait, first you want to cut him off, and now you want him to take your place?" Gideon asked, confused.

"Sometimes, even kings are wrong," his father admitted, grimacing.

Both of his sons recoiled and stared at him.

"I am so sorry to both of you. Gabe, I should never have asked you to sacrifice your family for the crown. I am proud of you for standing firm."

Gabe swallowed hard and nodded his head in acceptance.

Sensing his brother's emotions, Gideon reached over and gave him a quick shoulder squeeze.

"Gideon," the king continued, "I apologize for not getting help sooner for your mother. The situation with Eden should never have happened."

Gideon now found himself the one too choked up to speak. It took him a moment to tune back into his father's words.

" . . . we can only hope and pray that she has sons."

"What? Why?" Gideon asked, his voice sharp. "Eden?"

"Your brother will eventually be king, not just prince regent."

Gideon nodded his understanding.

"But you and your sons will be his heirs," the king concluded.

Gideon sighed. "Do you know how many kingdoms have fallen from that archaic rule? We need to change things."

"Besides, is Eden even talking to you?" his brother asked.

Gideon wondered how he could feel love for his brother one minute and want to punch him in the face the next. His vision of his brother bent over with blood squirting from his face was distracting enough that once again his father had to repeat himself.

"Gideon, are you listening?" his father asked.

"Yes, sir," Gideon asked, hoping he had not missed anything.

"Eden is on her way back to the island."

Gideon's heart jumped at the words, but he needed clarification. "I thought she was in England for engagements," he ventured cautiously.

"I ordered her back for her wedding to you."

13

EDEN, TRAGIC RETURN

I noted my father's silence as he gazed out the plane window into the clouds rolling against it. He was a quiet man usually, but this was a different type of quiet—disapproving, unhappy. I understood his dismay. He had arranged for me to get away from Gideon for my own sanity, but he had no power to gainsay the king who had ordered us to return to the island. He also had no authority as my father since that was a secret too. There was no way to speak openly of our thoughts on a private plane with royal guard members.

With a sigh I turned on my phone screen only to be greeted by articles about Asier's return to the island. I was happy for Lily and Prince Gabriel, but I did wonder about Asier's family. The news was that his adoptive parents had died but I thought he had siblings in that family and aunts and uncles as well. They lost not only his adoptive parents but Asier as well.

Of course, I uncomfortably thought of my own unknown birth family and Dr. Brown. Now my mood matched the clouds outside, gray and churning without a ray of light. I forced myself to stop the emotional spiral and think. It was right after the news broke that Prince Gabriel would not be removed from the line of succession that the king ordered my return to the island. Most likely the events were connected but I couldn't see how. I was also annoyed that I had not been trusted with news of Asier's return when it was already public, and confined to my suite with no internet access. Lily showing up at my door with Asier in tow was a bit of a shock. It was demoralizing to find out the way I did. Frustrated, I decided to distract myself by making small talk.

"Are you coming back from an event?" I politely asked the guard seated next to me.

"No," the guard replied. I think her name was Talia Gold and like the other five or so guards on the plane, she was completely impersonal.

"Hmmm," I drawled out. "It is unusual for us to have so many guards. Is there a situation we need to be apprised of?"

RG Gold looked down and away. There was something I should have known.

"I only follow orders," she replied.

I really wanted to shake the answer out of her, but I managed to nod civilly. Part of a royal education is learning to look unaffected when you want to scream madly. So, I put in my headphones, closed my eyes, and let island music counteract my nerves until I felt a hand on my arm. Opening my eyes, I saw it belonged to my father. I took out my earphones.

"We'll assess the situation when we arrive," my father said. He opened his mouth to speak again but then closed it. He hated my habit of wearing headphones to listen to music, thinking I lacked situational awareness. I knew he was right in general, but I did not think it was that big of a deal on a plane. He must have agreed because he did not say anything else.

I nodded to show I understood his words. There was not much we could say with an audience. My heart was pleased, however, that even though he could not openly declare he was my father, he showed his love for me in quieter ways, like getting me off the island on a pretext before I completely melted down over Gideon, love and frustration draining my brain of coherent, rational thought.

Even with the calming music, though, my thoughts were like jumping beans, and I barely restrained myself from pacing the aisle. I was not sure what I wanted to do.

Shaking my head, I pulled out a ball of red yarn. As soon as we had landed in England, I noticed a yarn shop in the airport. It had been nicely decorated with knitted and crocheted scarves, hats, gloves, sweaters, shawls, and dresses. My eyes had been drawn to a bowl filled with balls of bulky yarn. I had picked up the red ball and immediately thought of knitting a scarf, not because I needed one but to keep my hands busy. It was only as we were on our way back to the island that I actually started working on said scarf.

The first row was a snarled mess, so I put the project aside but then pulled it out again and started over. My stitches came out more evenly, and I let the repetitive motion—along with the music—calm me. Unbidden came an image of me wrapping a red scarf around Gideon's neck, creating a circle within which we existed for each other. I felt a nudge against my feet, and my startled eyes met my father's gaze. He nodded discreetly toward RG Gold.

"I'm sorry, did you say something?" I asked, finally putting the headphones away.

"It does get boring after a while, doesn't it?" she asked.

"Huh?" Seeing her eyes on the yarn, I realized she had been speaking about the knitting I was no longer doing.

"I like it," I said with a shrug. "My mind was on other things."

She assessed me a little too long, and I awkwardly smiled and put the yarn away. There was no way, I hoped, that she could guess what—or who, rather—I had been thinking about.

As the plane flew closer to the island's airport, the guards got up and stood closer to the front of the plane. I could still see them from where I sat, and from the frowns on their faces, they did not look pleased. RG Gold must have been designated as the spokesperson because she headed back to us with a determined look on her face.

"When we land, we'll need to move quickly. Just grab your purse and keep moving. Someone else will grab your luggage."

As we flew beneath the clouds the island became more visible, the aerial view catching my breath like it always did when I returned to the island. The curves of the island, the colorful fields, and the mountains protecting the Red Palace were like satiny ribbons wrapping gently around my wrists to lead me home, even if the home was only temporary. I leaned closer to the window. As I felt the wheels touch down in a smooth glide, I frowned.

"We are not at a gate," I said. But as I spoke, my eyes caught a line of shiny black vehicles with the royal emblem. They raced toward us. My heart sped up as well, wondering if Gideon had come to pick us up.

"Is someone from the royal family landing too?" I asked as I looked at RG Gold.

A flicker of irritation crossed her face. "The cars are for you and Mr. Mann. Remember, you can't pause. As soon as the door opens, you'll need to move quickly down the steps and into the middle vehicle." The sternness in her voice took me aback.

"We've got it," my father said.

I stepped down as quickly as possible in the heels I'd not had the foresight to replace earlier with more comfortable shoes. A roaring noise had my head turning, but Mr. Mann's hand on my back urged me to keep going.

Once everyone was loaded in, the cars zoomed off quickly, but instead of moving directly to Green Street, they moved toward the airport.

"Why are we—" the guard in our car started to ask the driver.

"There is an accident at the intersection, so the cars need to merge onto the street past the accident."

By now, we had reached the regular transportation pick-up section of the airport, except no cars were able to move due to the mass of people. I squinted to see if they were media or just curious travelers, when it registered that a rock was spinning in the air straight toward us. My head was shoved unceremoniously between my knees by Mr. Mann as the car went even faster but backward. I eventually felt the car spin around and move forward, but Mr. Mann's hand was still firmly on my neck. I dared not move.

"You are safe," the guard finally said. "We'll need to circle back to Green Street."

I breathed a sigh of relief as I cautiously sat up, noting no broken glass as I rubbed my neck. I looked at my father, a question in my eyes.

He reached out to me but then retracted his hand, a pained expression on his face. I swallowed the lump in my throat as my eyes followed his hand. Now that we were back on the island, we were no longer father and daughter but workers serving the monarchy. Before we could speak, I heard Gideon's voice on the car speaker, cursing.

"What if the rock had hit her head?" he yelled.

"Sir—" the guard began.

"Did you call every media outlet?" Gideon continued. "There were flashes going off everywhere in the footage I saw."

"Sir—" the guard began again.

"Get her to the plaza," Gideon commanded and hung up.

"I was also in the car," my father mumbled.

I patted his shoulder sympathetically and felt my wrist buzz. It was a message from Gideon. *I'm glad you're back. If it were up to me, you would already know what is going on, but I've been overruled. As soon as the announcement is over, can we talk?*

I texted, *Okay.* I noted that he had framed his question as a request and not a command.

At my father's questioning look, I shrugged. Gideon had given me no real information. He was right about one thing, though. We probably should have already talked about whatever this upcoming event was.

As we drove, the rain that had been threatening started first lightly then in torrents.

Finally, we arrived at the Golden Bowl Plaza, where the annual Supreme Fighter Championships were held. It was unusual for the royal family to make announcements live at the Plaza but the venue was the largest on the island as far as number of seats. For this day's announcement, it was filled and surrounded by citizens with blue umbrellas and see-through gold rain ponchos. The royal guard drove underground as opposed to trying to drive through the crowd to get closer.

Underground a few folks milled about here and there but nothing like the sheer number of people above ground. The driver was able to get close to the elevator, and my father and I rushed to get in it while a guard held the doors.

As the doors started to close, a masked figure jumped in front but disappeared as the doors closed with a strange noise. I breathed a sigh of relief as the elevator jerked upwards but then something hot splashed into my face. Wiping my face, I barely noticed the red smearing on my fingertips because my father jerked and grunted. I turned to look as he was falling to the floor, blood gurgling from his mouth.

I screamed and placed my hand over my mouth as a guard knelt and opened my father's suit jacket to reveal a blood-soaked white dress shirt. I fell on my knees as two guards frantically worked to stanch the bleeding. One pulled off his shirt and placed it over the wound and pressed down.

"Please hang on, please hang on . . ." I whispered in a litany, my blood-tinged hands clasped wetly in front of me.

"Eden!" I looked up into Gideon's shocked face. The elevator had opened, and Gideon stood right in front of me with EMTs on either side of him.

"Sir," a voice said, and Gideon moved to let the EMTs place my father on a stretcher and rush him out. A guard ran with them as his hands were still trying to staunch the bleeding.

I awkwardly stood up. "I need to follow them to the hospital."

Gideon gently hugged me while quietly talking to those around us. I did not follow anything he said, anxious to get to the hospital. I pulled back to tell him I had to go but one of the emergency techs came up to check me over.

"I'm fine, I need to . . ." I started backing away.

"It's not her blood," Gideon interjected as he stepped back with me. Somehow, he had gotten hold of some wipes and used them to gently wipe the blood off my face and hands. By the time he was done the tech had moved on. Gideon took my hand and led me down the steps to a waiting car. Quickly, I realized we were headed toward the palace and not the hospital.

"Is he . . ." I could not bring myself to ask if my father was dead.

"I had him taken to the palace to be treated by the royal medical staff," Gideon explained.

"But why?"

He sighed and pulled me closer so one hand clasped mine while his other arm was around my shoulders. "The announcement today is that my father is temporarily stepping down to help the queen recover and putting my brother in charge."

"That's pretty big news," I said, but my words were flat, consumed as I was with worry.

"Well, if my brother becomes acting king or eventually the permanent king, any heirs he has would have to come through me." He was looking at me like he was willing me to understand. But I did not.

"With Asier's return, would not he be your brother's heir?"

Gideon shook his head. "In order to have Gabe remain in the line of succession, we implied that Asier would be a non-heir."

"Your heirs would be his then?" My worry laden brain finally caught on to the implications.

"Is that the most important thing at the moment?" I continued softly.

He did not respond.

After we arrived at the palace, I rushed to the infirmary, only to be told that Mr. Mann was in surgery. After one hour and then two hours passed with no word, I felt the walls closing in on me.

Walking out of the infirmary, I headed to one of the palace gardens. Outside, I realized the unusual winter rain had become snow. Flakes coated my eyelashes until it was hard to see, and I closed my eyes. Yet, I did not move, the chill almost a welcome reprieve from the fearful infirmary air.

And then abruptly there was no snow falling on me. I blinked my eyes open and found an umbrella over my head, held by Gideon. Snowflakes fell around us both.

"He's made it out of surgery."

14

GIDEON, A PROPOSAL

"Saved America wants Eden back," Gideon informed Mr. Mann as he stood by his recovery bedside.

"That's the intel?" Mr. Mann asked, managing to look formidable even while recovering from being shot.

Gideon nodded.

"Is there a reason?"

"We surmise that there was a competitive interest in Eden while she was at the school. Our sources indicate that Mrs. Grey from her old school in Saved America is involved. Besides . . ." Gideon paused.

"What is it?" Mr. Mann asked.

"Eden's reaction to your getting shot has some folks speculating on the nature of your relationship," Gideon replied.

Both men laughed at the absurdity before returning to more serious business.

"Why was I shot?"

"Seven apparently has a successor group, Eight."

Mr. Mann snorted. "How original. What do they want?"

"Chaos," Gideon replied. "They knew there was a lot of speculation over the Asier situation and wanted to exploit that to cast a negative image on the family."

"Especially on a day that the king was set to make an important announcement," Mr. Mann commented. "They were behind the airport incidents?"

Gideon nodded. "Some of the protestors were flown in but we are checking to see if any are from the island." He watched as Mr. Mann leaned back and closed his eyes while grimacing in pain.

"Do you need me to call the doctor?" Gideon inquired, concerned.

"You plan to marry her?" Mr. Mann responded, reopening his eyes but frowning.

Gideon nodded, wanting to see how Mr. Mann responded.

"For whose sake?" Mr. Mann asked. "You don't love her."

Taken aback, Gideon replied. "But I do."

"Let me ask you something. If a man described how much he loved his horse but then forgot to feed it so that it starved, would you say the man loved his horse?"

"Of course not," Gideon replied, guilt making him curt. "Eden is not a horse, and I am not the man in your analogy."

"Why don't you wait until you resolve your differences?" Mr. Mann asked.

"I can't wait. The situation with my bro—" And with those words, Gideon saw the trap he had fallen into. "Look, two things can be true at once. I messed up with Eden, and I plan to make it right because I love her. And the family is looking for me to get married as soon as possible."

"You are rushing this process," Mr. Mann replied before hissing as pain went through him. He waved off Gideon's efforts to get assistance, but his voice was unsteady when he continued speaking. "I've been shot, it's painful."

"But there's medication . . ." Gideon started, alarmed by the strain lines on Mr. Mann's face.

"Eden has choices too. Frankly, there are better options for her than to be your bride. And you know it too."

After leaving his uncomfortable visit with Eden's father, Gideon went in search of Eden. He did not have much time as she was due to visit her father soon. He found her in the family room by the atrium, sitting in a rocking chair that had been added. She wore pale pink, almost beige jeans with a pink top as she knitted a red scarf, the sun from the atrium catching glints of gold from her curled hair. *His dream come to life in front of him.* She looked up when he entered, and a smile started to form, but then she remembered and looked down, her hands stilling.

The distance between them had never felt so vast. The girl of his literal dreams sat in front of him, and he loved her. But he had killed her feelings for him. Unbidden, his mind recalled the image of her stricken face smeared with her father's blood, her hands held up as if pleading for her father's life. He fingered the box with the ring in his pocket. Living his life without her was simply not an option for him. But in order for her to choose him he would have to choose her.

After walking across the room, he sat next to her chair as she turned to face him, her eyes wary. "What do you need from me in order for me to regain your trust? To agree to marry me?"

Eden sadly shook her head, reaching out a palm to cup his face. "Let me ask you something: if your father was not stepping down and Asier was not returned, would you even be here?"

Gideon maintained her gaze. "Those situations only expedited what we both want." He cupped the side of her face with his own hand so that they held on to each other, their faces only inches apart.

"We need time to either choose each other – or walk away," Eden whispered. "I will not agree to marry you as an expediency."

Relief flooded Gideon. She hadn't rejected him outright.

But then footsteps could be heard approaching. James and Luke appeared at the door with one of the family attorneys. Both Gideon and Eden stood up, alarmed. James and Luke rarely came to the family's private rooms. They were even more alarmed when another figure entered. It was Jack Holt, the man placed by the royal family at the Joseph Hyde School for Exceptional Girls.

"Mr. Holt!" Eden exclaimed. "What are you doing here?"

"Saving you again," he said, one eyebrow raised.

"Saving her from what?" Gideon asked, pulling Eden closer to him.

"There is a delegation from Saved America," James began, his voice winded. "They are asking to extradite Eden for leaving their country without authorization and, well, murder, sir."

"Murder of whom?" Eden asked in astonishment.

"Your mother," Luke replied.

Eden gasped and swayed.

Gideon squeezed Eden tighter. "But she is a Seahorse Island citizen."

James shook his head. "They appear willing to dispute her citizenship in international court."

"Marriage would prohibit their ability to bring a citizenship case," Jack Holt said, his eye on Gideon's arm around Eden's waist. "Then you would only need to handle the murder case." He looked to the attorney for confirmation, who nodded.

Gideon looked at Eden, noting the look of shock on her face. He knelt, one hand holding on to her arm, the other reaching into his pocket.

"You asked for time, but time has slipped away leaving only this moment. I have loved you imperfectly, caused you great hurt and pain, and forgot to focus on the truth. The truth is I love you with a love deeper than the ocean, and I promise to stand by your side no matter what comes, to not be swayed by others. Will you marry me?" he asked.

AUTHOR'S NOTE

Thank you for reading CHOOSING EDEN—*Book Two: When Choosing Is Not A Choice!* I hope you enjoyed the continuation of Eden and Gideon's story.

If you want to get updates about new releases, please visit my website: https://www.LisaLeeWrites.com. I love to hear from readers, so please feel free to leave a comment!

If you enjoyed this story, please leave a review and tell your friends!

ACKNOWLEDGMENTS

Thank you, God, for giving me the words to express my imagination.
Thank you, David, Faith and Solomon for your encouragement, love,
and faith that I would actually finish this story.
Thank you, Christina Schrunk, for your thoughtful and amazing
editing.
Thank you, Patricia Moffett, for such an imaginative and delightful
cover design.
Thank you, Krista Burdine and Faith Lee, for proofreading and catching
the errors that almost slipped through.
And finally, thank you reader for taking the time to read this story.

www.ingramcontent.com/pod-product-compliance
Lightning Source LLC
Chambersburg PA
CBHW020951180626
46814CB00003B/1034